"Don't lie to me."

Julian stared at Holly as he spoke. "You stole the goblets."

Holly sank onto the edge of the bed and put all she had into looking terribly hurt and confused. "I don't understand— Why would I steal anything from you? I'm a successful storyteller. I have a reputation to maintain."

"Give it up, Holly," Julian bent over and placed his hands on his thighs, steadying himself as he looked straight into her eyes. "Where did you stash them?"

"Really," she said, leaning back on her elbows. A dumb move. Her robe fell open and exposed more cleavage than she'd intended. Pretending not to notice, she continued. "Search my room, if you want. Search my van. Search me—"

A mistake. She realized it too late. Julian's mouth was on hers the moment the words were out. *This*, thought Holly, *is one way to catch a thief....*

Carla Neggers knows how to tell a story—as her many fans will attest. But this talented, prolific author has always admired the oral tradition of storytelling, the sheer magic of the spoken word. So Carla created Holly Wingate Paynter, heroine of *Finders Keepers* and teller of tall tales *extraordinaire*! And where did Carla get the inspiration for fictitious Milbrook, Vermont, the historic mill town setting of her sixth Temptation? Where else but the old millpond that served as the swimming hole of her childhood!

Books by Carla Neggers

HARLEQUIN TEMPTATION
108–CAPTIVATED
162–TRADE SECRETS
190–FAMILY MATTERS
208–ALL IN A NAME
236–A WINNING BATTLE

Don't miss any of our special offers. Write to us at the following address for information on our newest releases.

Harlequin Reader Service
901 Fuhrmann Blvd., P.O. Box 1397, Buffalo, NY 14240
Canadian address: P.O. Box 603,
Fort Erie, Ont. L2A 5X3

Finders Keepers

CARLA NEGGERS

Harlequin Books

TORONTO • NEW YORK • LONDON
AMSTERDAM • PARIS • SYDNEY • HAMBURG
STOCKHOLM • ATHENS • TOKYO • MILAN

Published November 1989

ISBN 0-373-25375-3

DISCOVERY OF PAUL REVERE GOBLETS STIRS UP CENTURY-OLD SCANDAL

Millbrook, Vermont: Scandal revisited this picturesque New England village today when a member of one of its oldest and most respected families announced his discovery of a pair of sterling-silver goblets crafted by Paul Revere and reported missing a hundred years ago.

Julian Danvers Stiles, vice president of Mill Brook Post and Beam, manufacturers of high-quality housing kits, made the discovery in the dirt cellar of the Danvers House, the former president's house of the now-defunct Millbrook Preparatory Academy. The Stiles family recently purchased the buildings and hundred acres of the prestigious former boys' school.

"I have no idea how the goblets got there," Stiles said.

Himself an alumnus of the academy, Stiles admitted the discovery of the goblets did challenge the town's long-cherished version of the events of that cold winter night in 1889 when Zachariah Wingate and the Revere goblets disappeared.

"He was from an impoverished family up on the river," Stiles explained, "but he'd been given a scholarship to attend the academy. In his senior year, he decided to 'repay' the scholarship by presenting the school with the prized pair of goblets."

Zachariah Wingate's schoolmasters—including two of Julian Stiles's own ancestors—accused the boy of having stolen the goblets out of misguided pride. He was promptly expelled.

Two nights later, Zachariah left town. In the morning, the goblets were discovered gone from the academy safe located in the Danvers House.

"People just assumed Zachariah stole them back," Stiles said.

Does the discovery of the disputed goblets exonerate Zachariah Wingate? "Absolutely not," Stiles said. "There's no way a family as poor as his was could have gotten its hands on a valuable pair of goblets."

One of Zachariah's descendants might argue with his conclusion, he admitted. "But no one knows what happened to him after he left Millbrook, and a Wingate hasn't stepped foot in this part of Vermont in a century."

1

HOLLY WINGATE PAYNTER leaned her crowbar against the paint-chipped doorjamb and warily eyed the floor of the cold, dark master bedroom. A leaky ceiling and years of abandonment and neglect had left their mark. It didn't look good. Holly considered skipping the bedroom, but she'd prowled through every other room in the woefully dilapidated Danvers House, soaking up its creepy atmosphere.

She scanned the room with her powerful flashlight and frowned as she considered possible routes. She wasn't particularly worried, just didn't want to accidentally leave her footprints in the rotten wood. Being a Wingate, she wasn't exactly at the Danvers House by invitation. Best to avoid any careless mistakes.

Since crossing the town line into Millbrook, Vermont, an hour ago, she had been uncharacteristically cautious. She simply didn't know what to expect. Still, lightning hadn't struck at the arrival of a Wingate in town. Her van tires hadn't started smoking. Her stomach hadn't rebelled on her. And neither Grandpa Zachariah Wingate nor Great-grandpa Zachariah Wingate had come back to life to choke her for not heeding their advice that Vermont was no place for a Wingate.

In fact, nothing had happened. As Holly had driven out to the defunct Millbrook Preparatory Academy for Boys, the winter afternoon had remained startlingly bright and clear, the rolling hills of the Green Mountains outlined against as blue a sky as she'd ever seen. No question, it was beautiful country. Nevertheless, she'd be shed of it just as soon as she was finished with the business that had brought her there.

The *Wingate* goblets. Crafted by Paul Revere and presented by him, in gratitude, to the first Zachariah Wingate two hundred years ago. They'd been in the family until Great-grandpa Wingate's foolish pride had gotten in the way—and elitist Jonathan Stiles and Edward Danvers had assumed the worst about an impoverished Wingate.

Holly meant to restore the goblets to their intended place as a Wingate family heirloom. Since she was the last of Zachariah's direct descendants, the duty fell to her. There was no one else to do the job.

She shivered and slowly stepped onto the precarious floorboards, then carefully made her way into the drafty, unheated room. It was forty degrees in southern Vermont. That seemed to delight the folks on the local radio station Holly'd listened to in her van, but she was used to a balmier climate. She had been in central Florida when she'd read the wire-service article on the discovery of the goblets in the Danvers House cellar. She'd memorized every word. Had cursed Julian Danvers Stiles on her mad three-day trip north. *A Wingate hasn't stepped foot in this part of Vermont in a century.* As if one wouldn't dare.

"Well, here I am, buster."

But her words sounded hollow and not particularly convincing in the big, empty wreck of a house. It had done her soul good to find the once elegant Danvers House so hopelessly deteriorated. She wondered what kind of incorrigible optimist Julian Danvers Stiles was to think he could convert such a dump into a decent restaurant—or anything.

She stopped suddenly, certain she'd heard something. A growl almost. A guard dog? No, she'd been sneaking around for a good forty minutes; a guard dog would have tracked her down by now. But she was sure she'd heard something.

Feeling uneasy in the strange building, she glanced back longingly at her crowbar; all she had for immediate protection was her flashlight. And her mouth, she supposed. Grandpa Wingate would have told her to trust her powers of persuasion. "There isn't any trouble," he used to tell everyone, "my granddaughter can't talk herself out of."

Or get herself into, he'd add privately, to her alone.

But first she had to have someone to persuade, and Holly had no idea *what* was downstairs.

"Hell, look at this mess," a distinctly solid male voice snarled in disgust. "Beth? Are you in here?"

Sweat poured down Holly's back, despite the cold. She wondered if she wouldn't rather deal with a guard dog than whatever none-too-pleased individual was downstairs.

"Abby, David?" he hollered. "You in here? Who made this mess?"

Oh, sure, Holly thought. *I'll just yell down, "Hey, it was me, a nice lady from Texas who couldn't resist*

*using her trusty crowbar to peel a couple of boards off
that window there and crawling in for a look around."*

Breaking and entering, it was called. All in a good
cause, but this was Millbrook, she was a Wingate and
whoever was downstairs was in no mood. Holly kept
her mouth shut and didn't move.

"Kids?"

Nope. Holly was thirty-three. Even as a kid she
hadn't been much of a kid.

She heard a creak and took hope, thinking he might
just leave. All she had to do was hang in there another
few minutes, not move, not scratch, not make a sound.
But her hope faded when the creak was followed by the
sound of a hammer expertly tackling one nail and then
another.

"All right," he said, obviously pleased with himself.
"Whoever you are, you'd better come out now. I've
nailed you in. Only way out is through the front door,
with me."

Ha! She'd jump out the window first! All she had to
do was lunge for her crowbar, smash through a window and jump. The snow would cushion her fall. Even
if she broke an ankle, she could threaten to sue the bastard for provoking such an act of desperation. But she
wouldn't break anything. She'd scramble to her feet,
beat a path to her van and screech out of town. No one
would be the wiser.

She could almost hear Grandpa Wingate saying, "I
told you so."

Maybe she should have ignored the item about the
goblets and continued her winter wanderings in Florida.

Not sure what the intruder downstairs was up to now, Holly gritted her teeth and switched off her flashlight. A thin shaft of light angled into the dark room through a crack in two boards over one tall window.

"You wouldn't by any chance be driving a dark green van," the voice said under her feet, "Texas license plate F6H-421?"

Startled, Holly had trouble keeping her precarious footing on the pine-board floor, which was in horrendous shape from years of neglect, leaks and vandalism. If she moved, the man downstairs would hear her. *Who was he?* Her only consolation was that he couldn't be the owner. Men like Julian Danvers Stiles stayed out of crumbling old houses, even if they owned them.

But that bit in the newspaper indicated he'd found the goblets himself. If he'd dig around down in a dirt cellar, why wouldn't he check out a trespasser?

It wasn't the sort of question she wanted to answer, so she didn't.

Inexpert snoop that she was, she'd made a halfhearted attempt to hide her van, parking alongside a snowbank and a stand of pines. Obviously she could have saved herself the trek across the blustery football field. While trying to keep herself from freezing in that "balmy" forty-degree air, she'd entertained herself imagining generations of preppy boys out there mucking it up. She'd wondered if the sparkling white in their blue-and-white football uniforms had ever gotten dirty.

"Vermont's a long way from Texas."

Don't you know it, Holly thought. She concentrated on keeping still—and her mouth shut, which was against her nature. Imagining comebacks wasn't nearly as satisfying as saying them out loud. She always preferred to say her piece.

"Okay, have it your way. I know every inch of this house. Wherever you're hiding, I'll find you."

Who was hiding?

Holly's notion of self-preservation didn't include standing in the middle of a dark, unheated bedroom on the second floor of an abandoned house built by a Danvers while waiting for some strange man to come fetch her.

Hoping his movement underneath her would cover any noise she made, she bit her lip and started gingerly from her position over a thick beam out onto a wide circle of rotting, weakened pine floorboards. It was the quickest route to her crowbar. Since speed was of the essence, she had to chance it.

Snow had gotten into her brand-new gum shoes; her feet were cold and wet, a little numb. But she could feel the floor begin to give way under them.

"Oh, no," she groaned softly, even as one foot sank into the rotten wood.

She tried yanking it free, but shifted her weight onto her other foot, sinking it. Her flashlight went flying, and she frantically reached for something to grab.

There was nothing.

Underneath her the floor swayed like a hammock. Then the rotted laths collapsed and the ceiling plaster gave way, and she plunged into thin air.

She yelled, not giving a damn who heard her.

An instant later she landed hard on her left side. Her ski jacket—white with rose accents, purchased at an outlet sale less than twenty-four hours earlier—cushioned her fall to some degree, but not enough. The impact knocked the wind out of her. Cursing and groaning, she fought to catch her breath and made a quick check of various body parts. Her left hip ached. Her behind ached. Her right wrist ached. Her functional kelly-green gloves—they were the only ones left on sale—had spared her hands cuts and scratches. Her hat, bright red with a multicolored pom-pom, another sale-bin castoff, was no longer atop her strawberry-colored curls.

Confident nothing was broken, she started coughing and spitting every manner of disgusting thing that might be trapped in a two-hundred-year-old ceiling. She had visions of discovering a bat or mouse skeleton lodged in her throat.

The male voice that had caused all this trouble sounded from somewhere within the cloud of dust her fall had created. "What the hell's going on here?"

I fell, you idiot! Holly quickly checked her anger, frustration and delayed fear. The bastard had had no business goading her like that! She'd never have fallen if he'd just left her alone! But common sense warned her now wasn't the time to argue those points.

Now, she thought, was the time to come up with a good story.

Picking bits of plaster from her hair, she sat up and blinked. Dust stung her eyes, but her vision was still a sharp twenty-twenty. As the dust settled, she had no trouble making out the tall, plaster-covered, unhappy male figure looming over her. He had thick dark hair, a straight nose and this morning's beard on his square Yankee jaw. His eyes were vividly green against the white film of plaster covering his face. Strongly built, he wore torn jeans, a heavy black mock-turtleneck and battered boots. No coat was in evidence. Hell, Holly thought, it was *forty* outside. Who needed a coat?

Just her luck to fall at the feet of a mountain man Yankee.

Yet better him, she supposed, than a snot-nosed Danvers or Stiles—or Julian Danvers Stiles himself. He was two Wingate enemies rolled into one. She didn't need *that* kind of aggravation right now. She'd have to deal with the owner of the Danvers House sooner or later, but preferably not in her present condition.

"Well?" the troublemaker demanded again.

He must be a carpenter, Holly concluded. His stake in the once-magnificent old house would be purely professional. Except he'd called out names, she recalled. Beth, Abby, David. Who were they? Rising slowly, Holly winced. She thought it prudent to look as if she were in more pain than she actually was. Scare the guy a little. Make him wonder, *Lord, what'll Julian Stiles do when he finds out I scared this poor tourist from Texas and made her fall through the ceiling?*

With a small, brave groan, she said, "I fell."

"So I see."

His tone was dry and not altogether sympathetic. He seemed unconcerned about her or even his own position. That didn't suit Holly at all.

"You're all right?" he asked, disinterested, as he brushed plaster chips off his shoulder.

"I . . . I think so."

Her hesitation had no effect. "Good."

Obviously he'd already assumed she was just fine. He wasn't even remotely worried. Even when she stumbled a little, not making too big a deal, just enough for him to notice, he just stood there. Her general annoyance with him increased. "And you?" she asked sharply. "Are *you* all right?"

He shrugged. "I got out of the way."

How chivalrous. "I guess that was smart."

"I had no idea what was coming down on top of me. If I'd known . . ." He paused, his vivid eyes taking in all one-hundred-fifteen pounds of her. "I guess I could have caught you."

"You might have broken your arms," she said lightly, suddenly feeling quite warm, a first since her arrival in New England. A welcome gust of brisk air blew in from the open front door behind her in the entry. "Thanks for your concern. I'll just be heading on out now—"

"Whoa, there. How 'bout telling me what you're doing here?"

She thought about her crowbar and flashlight upstairs and wondered if she should work them into her story. He'd find them at some point, but by then she could be long gone from Millbrook, Vermont. She didn't plan to stay long. Wasn't a lucky place for Wingates.

"Oh—well, it's a long story, actually."

"Give me a shortened version. Let's start with how you got in."

"That's obvious. Through the window."

"How'd you pry off the plywood?"

She shrugged. "Crowbar."

"Ah-huh."

"My name's Holly, by the way. Holly Paynter."

She'd have preferred using a fake name, but if he had her license plate number, he could get her name. And a good story always wove in elements of the truth.

"I'm from Houston," she went on cheerfully, peeling off her gloves and dusting herself here and there. "Down home an abandoned building's fair game. Guess it's the same up here, huh?"

"No," he replied without humor, "it's not."

As far as she knew, it wasn't in Houston, either. She affected good-natured surprise. "No kidding?"

He didn't smile back at her. "No kidding."

What a sourpuss, Holly thought. "I'll keep that in mind next time I have call to slip inside an abandoned building in New England—"

"This one's posted with several dozen No Trespassing and Danger signs."

"So I noticed. What're you doing here?"

"Ms Paynter, you had to have known you were trespassing."

She hadn't thought he'd answer her question. "Sorry. Live and learn, I guess. Look, if you'll excuse me, I'll just be on my way. I'm not used to this cold weather. I've got to get back to my van and warm up my toes."

She spotted her hat hanging on a lath next to the gaping hole in the ceiling. What a mess he'd caused her to make. Holly didn't look forward to crossing that bleak tundra of a football field with a bare head, but now wasn't the time to be wimpish. And she wasn't about to cross in front of him to retrieve her hat, such as it was.

She began edging her way toward the front door. "Too bad we had to meet under such circumstances, but I guess that's how it goes sometimes. Nice meeting you, Mr...."

"Stiles. Julian Stiles."

"Hellfire."

"I beg your pardon?"

"Nothing. Just thinking out loud." *I'm doomed—doomed! He's supposed to be a stodgy old Yankee! Not half a day in Millbrook and I'm already up to my neck in boiling water!* But she managed to give a nonchalant sigh. "Really, I'm going to freeze if I stand here another minute."

"You won't freeze," he said.

She wondered if maybe she looked as hot and trapped as she felt. "Sorry about the mess, but this place is such a wreck, I don't think it makes a whole lot of difference." She was serious: he already had to contend with peeling plaster, leaks, filthy wallpaper, rusty sinks, crumbling fireplaces, cracked windows, nasty words spray painted on the walls. What was a little hole in the ceiling? She went on, "You know the owner, give him my apologies."

"I am the owner."

She feigned surprise. "You?"

"That's right. I'm the one who boarded up the window you pried open and posted the signs you ignored."

His green eyes glared at her, and now she could see the Danvers and Stiles devil dancing behind them. Driving up to Vermont from warm, sunny Florida, Holly had wondered what Julian Stiles would be like. She'd imagined a slick preppy type who knew how to turn a fast profit and didn't give a damn about a family's honor. A man who'd think the descendants of Zachariah Wingate had forgotten about the outrageous lie that had driven their great-grandfather out of his hometown. If those damned snobs from the Millbrook Preparatory Academy for Boys had thought to ask, any Wingate would have told them Zachariah hadn't blown town with Revere sterling-silver goblets.

Grandpa Wingate had told Holly the whole story when she was eight. When she was twenty-five and the academy, its endowment depleted and enrollment down, had gone under, she and Grandpa had toasted its demise.

"You know," Julian Stiles said, "you could have been killed."

"I wasn't."

He took a step toward her, the stranger who'd invaded his territory. If not overtly menacing, he seemed determined to stake out his rights. He would be that way about the goblets, too, Holly realized—suspicious, protective, possessive. Too bad, though. They weren't his.

"You're not leaving without an explanation."

She laughed in disbelief. "Says who?"

"I can have you arrested for breaking and entering."

"Well, you'd look like a damn fool if you tried."

He almost smiled; she was sure of it. "Dare I ask why?"

"If you'd like." She didn't go on; she wasn't about to make this any easier on him. Also, she was stalling. She needed an extra minute to flesh out her story, make it believable. "You certainly don't have to ask me anything. You can go ahead and contact the police and wait and see—"

"No, I'm game." He bent one knee and settled back on his heels, his arms crossed on his chest. "Why would I be the one to look like a fool?"

Holly adopted an expression of unrelenting innocence and looked him straight in the eye. "Because everyone sympathizes with lost puppies."

"I was wondering if something like a lost puppy was going to come into this."

"Not one," Holly said gravely. "Two."

"Of course."

"I was driving by, you know, just checking out the scenery, when I spotted these two little guys on the side of the road. They were shivering like crazy, their tails between their legs—oh, they looked so forlorn."

"I'm sure they did."

"I'd say they were maybe twelve, fourteen weeks old."

"What breed?"

"Golden retriever mostly, I'd say."

"Difficult to resist."

His dry tone suggested he was humoring her against his better judgment, but Holly persevered. "*Impossible* to resist. I pulled over and went to grab them, but they charged off. Maybe they thought I was playing—or maybe they'd been abused by their owner and didn't trust humans. You know how puppies are. Anyway, I followed them here."

"To Danvers House," Stiles called.

"Is that what this place's called? Well, whatever. They got ahead of me and disappeared, and I just assumed they'd found a way inside here—a puppy-size hole they could squeeze into."

"And you just happened to have along your crowbar, so you pried open a window and climbed in."

He had her. Holly didn't wince or moan, just took a prudent step backward toward the entry. "More or less."

"You chased two stray puppies with a crowbar?"

"I believe in being prepared."

"That much," he said, "I do believe."

His eyes rested on her, seemed to soak her up, and for the first time since landing at his feet, Holly wondered what kind of picture she presented. Not a very good one, she supposed. Her chin-length strawberry hair was sticking out everywhere. She had grime all over her. No makeup on her small features—just plaster dust. Given the temperature and lack of heat in the place, her nose had to be red. She touched two fingers to her temple and felt blood coagulating around a scratch. How nice. But not enough to melt that cold Yankee Danvers-Stiles heart.

"Look," she said, "the rest—"

He cut her off with a shake of the head. "The rest is pure fiction, just like the beginning."

"Your word against mine."

"Fine. There were no puppies, Ms Paynter."

"Prove it."

"Okay. Let's walk outside and have a look at the tracks across the football field to your van. If I'm not mistaken—and I'm not—there'll be two sets: yours and mine."

Holly bit her lip and swallowed. Tracks?

"No puppy tracks," he said.

Tracks! She'd forgotten about the damned snow. Seeing the pried-open window, Julian Stiles had followed her tracks to her van. No wonder he'd found it.

She was going to have to bone up on New England life in winter. Remember details like the snow. Remember she was in enemy territory. Stay extra alert.

But those were tasks for later. Right now, her sole desire was to get herself off Julian Danvers Stiles's turf and out of his reach.

When the mouth fails, Holly thought, when cunning, imagination and alertness desert you—when, dammit, you're *caught*, there's only one sane option.

Your feet.

She about-faced, and bolted out the front door.

IF NOT FOR THE AMOUNT of work he had to do, Julian might have gone after Ms Holly Paynter of Houston, Texas. It wasn't the pried-open window or the mess she'd made of his ceiling so much that aroused his suspicions.

It was her eyes.

They were the most dishonest pair of blue eyes he'd ever seen.

Squinting in the bright sunlight streaming through the front door, he watched her slim figure race across the snow-covered football field. She had a head start and she was fast, even in the snow. Still, he figured he could have caught up with her before she slunk off in her van. But then what? Another tale, no doubt.

Lost puppies.

He went back into the living room and plucked her red hat from the lath where it hung by its multicolored pom-pom. Red hat, white-and-rose jacket, green gloves. Quite a mishmash.

Holly Paynter was a woman who bore watching.

Crushing her hat in one hand, Julian headed back to his Land Rover parked in front of the house. Off in the distance he could see the dark green Texas van pull out onto the road. He hoped he hadn't put such a scare into the strawberry-haired liar that she didn't pay attention to her driving. Somehow he didn't think so. For one thing, Holly Paynter didn't look like much intimidated her. For another, she seemed very committed to looking after her own skin.

He thought about following her, but didn't. He might have changed his mind, he supposed, if he suspected he'd never see her again. He was a thorough man. He didn't like loose ends. A strange woman crashing through his ceiling and then taking off without explanation—or with one that didn't wash—was a loose end.

Holly Paynter would be back.

Some things were just meant.

HOLLY WAS SO RELIEVED to have escaped the Danvers House relatively unscathed that she hardly noticed the bedraggled condition she was in until she arrived at Old Millbrook Common. There were two distinct parts of Millbrook, Vermont. Old Millbrook was where the original settlers had come in the early eighteenth century, building their homes and traditional white-steepled church around the still-pristine village green. The business district, a mile farther down the valley, had grown up around the Mill Brook—a river in Holly's book—during the early part of the Industrial Revolution. Many of its old sawmills and small factories had been converted into shops, boutiques and restaurants that were a favorite with tourists.

Every house around the snow-covered common was painted white with black shutters. Only the doors were of different colors—but all scrupulously subdued and colonial. Being of a recalcitrant, anti-Millbrook nature, Holly would have loved to have bought the biggest house there and painted it robin's egg blue. But she had to admit the sight was picturesque, even curiously peaceful. She had determined to keep her prejudices against Millbrook at bay, confident present-day residents would defend their town just as surely as their predecessors had. Julian Danvers Stiles already had a head start on them.

She found her way to the Windham House, where she had a reservation. It was one of the handsomest of the old colonials on the green, and exactly what Holly had pictured from its description in her New England guidebook. It had narrow white clapboards, black shutters, traditional landscaping and flagstone walks, and it was welcoming in a reserved Yankee manner.

Hair sticking out, covered with plaster dust, and still flushed from her near-disastrous adventure up the road, Holly doubted she looked like the average Windham House guest. She tried to dust off and spruce up, but there wasn't much she could do without soap and hot water. Finally she gave up. She hoped the proprietor of the Windham House had a soft spot for lost puppies.

Proprietress, Holly amended a few minutes later when Dorothy Windham answered the door. She was a distinguished-looking woman in late middle age, with strong features and graying, neatly coiffed hair. She wore a classic navy blazer and wool trousers, and she adored puppies.

"Of *course* I understand," she said when Holly started in about the puppy fiasco.

Guiltily Holly followed her into a cozy country kitchen, where sweet, yeasty smells permeated the air. The colors were all deep and rich, the furnishings practical and in quiet good taste. A large old-fashioned wood stove, a wrought-iron teakettle bubbling on top, occupied most of one wall, alongside an efficient work area with a butcher-block island. At the opposite end of the rectangular-shaped room was a pine trestle table overlooking the backyard where a score of birds were pecking at an array of feeders. The welcoming atmosphere and honey scents worked at unraveling Holly's tensed muscles and improving her spirits. As she'd hoped, the Windham House was proving to be just the refuge she'd need from the rest of Millbrook.

Dorothy Windham briefly explained that Holly had free run of the downstairs rooms and the grounds and should make herself at home. "I'll be serving tea at three-thirty—come if you like, but don't feel obligated."

Thanking her warmly, Holly listened as Dorothy gave her directions to the attic suite. "We added it just this fall," the older woman said. "My nephew Julian did most of the work. It's my favorite room now for winter."

Her nephew Julian? How many Julians could there be in a town the size of Millbrook?

"Anyone who isn't a Danvers in that town's a Stiles," Grandpa Wingate had told her, so long ago. "A Danvers founded the academy in the eighteenth century, and a Stiles endowed it in the nineteenth. You go to Millbrook, you got to deal with 'em. Myself, I'd just as soon not."

A wise choice, Holly thought.

Making her way upstairs, she congratulated herself on not being more specific on where she'd gone after her lost puppies and hoped Mrs. Windham and Julian Stiles didn't get a chance to compare notes on her. Right now, she was too tired and rattled to find another place to stay. And anyway, Millbrook or no, she wasn't used to tucking her tail between her legs and retreating.

The attic room had more charm than size, with slanted ceilings, tastefully papered walls, fresh white curtains, rag rugs and a painted floor. There was a double brass bed, an oak nightstand and dresser and a cross-stitched sampler hung above a small antique rocker. From the dormer window, Holly could look out on the backyard and bird feeders. Julian Danvers Stiles did physical work. Amazing.

Within minutes, she'd peeled off her dusty clothes and settled in a tub filled with hot, scented water. She had to get her bearings, think about her next step. No more bulldozing her way around. Patience wasn't her long suit, but she'd just have to be more careful.

An image of Julian Stiles's clear green eyes flashed into her mind. He was the kind of man who memorized other people's license plate numbers. How the devil was she going to get her goblets off him?

She'd just have to think of a way, that was all.

2

HOLLY AWOKE the next morning stiff and sore from her escapade in the Danvers House, but she felt altogether more in control of her situation. She would just have to cope with whatever the members of the Danvers and Stiles clans of Millbrook, Vermont, had to throw at her. She dressed Yankee style in hunter-green corduroys, a plaid flannel shirt over a turtleneck, warm socks and her gum shoes, which her trek through the snowy football field had conveniently cleaned of plaster dust.

She nodded with satisfaction at her reflection in the bathroom mirror. Texan by birth and nomad by choice, she was a New Englander by heritage. It wasn't anything she wanted to brag about, but she figured she could fool the entire population of Millbrook if she had to.

Except maybe Julian Stiles, who was top on her list of people she *needed* to fool.

What she could use now, she knew, was a dose of good luck. But since when had a Wingate ever been lucky? Luck wasn't their long suit and she was no exception. Everything she'd ever gotten in life, she'd had to work for. She didn't count on free lunches, inherited wealth and luck. She hoped Julian Stiles had forgotten all about yesterday's encounter. More likely it had only aroused his suspicions and he'd be on the lookout for her.

Well, she'd just have to be prepared. But that was a problem for later.

Postponing breakfast, she bundled up and headed outside, walking along a shoveled path across the Old Millbrook Common. The morning was cloudy and still relatively mild. The First Congregational Church on the common was one of the most photographed in New England. Holly could understand why. It was puritanically simple and stark white, its steeple the highest point in Old Millbrook. According to Grandpa Wingate, several Wingates had married in the church. *Before* the Zachariah Wingate scandal over the Revere goblets. For the moment, however, Holly was interested in the old Millbrook Burying Ground that adjoined the beautiful church.

A breeze was blowing and her cold ears reminded her of her missing hat and Julian Stiles. She repressed the thought of him and pushed open the wrought-iron gate, feeling a sense of overpowering peace descend upon her as she looked out at the thin stone slabs marking the graves, many two centuries old. The Wingates, she recalled from Grandpa's tales, would be toward the rear. She could see that no one had ventured along the paths among the gravestones since the last snow—perhaps since the *first* snow of the winter.

"How perfect," she murmured and stepped into a snowdrift up to her knees.

JULIAN POURED HIMSELF a mug of coffee from the thermal pot at his aunt's kitchen table. "I noticed a van outside with a Texas license plate," he said, sitting down. "New guest?"

Dorothy Windham was busily kneading a mound of dough for her famous sweet rolls. Converting her large house into a bed-and-breakfast had become a project for her after her husband's death a few years ago—an excuse for hanging on to the place, a way of going on and being whole without Roger. Julian, his brother, sister and cousins had all helped out in any way they could. Including, he thought, remaining on the alert for any unscrupulous guests, even ones with fetching strawberry hair and bright, lying eyes.

"Oh—yes, she arrived last night," Dorothy said absently. "Her name's Holly Paynter. She seems quite charming. She had a near-disaster getting here, however, when she tried to rescue a pair of lost puppies."

That damned Texan was relentless! "Aunt Doe . . ."

"I gave her the attic suite," she added blithely, but not one to gossip, changed the subject. "Julian, I've been meaning to ask you about those Revere goblets. Have you made any effort to investigate how they ended up buried in the Danvers House cellar?"

"Not really, no. Seems like a cold trail to me."

"It makes me uncomfortable to think we might have been wrong about Zachariah Wingate all these years."

Julian couldn't help but laugh. "You weren't even *born* when Zachariah was run out of town. What happened that night's not our responsibility—"

"Legally, perhaps not. But I believe we have a moral and ethical obligation to look into the matter."

"We?"

She sighed. Polite though she was, Dorothy was not one to back down. "You, then."

"I wouldn't even know where to begin."

Dorothy gently patted the mound of dough and covered it with a clean white cotton cloth. "You might call Felix Reichman."

"Who?"

An organized woman, she quickly produced her address book and jotted down a number and an address for a former American history professor recently retired to Millbrook. Julian promised he'd think about giving Reichman a call, but as far as he was concerned, what happened in 1889 was over; he owned the Danvers House, and the goblets were a case of finders keepers. But he understood his aunt's sensibilities—and her long view of local history.

With no graceful way to further interrogate his aunt about her new guest and her lost puppies, Julian took his mug and wandered through the downstairs rooms, hoping he might run into Holly and interrogate her himself. No such luck.

"Strange," he told his aunt, returning in frustration to the kitchen, "that someone from Texas would drive up to Vermont in winter."

"Flying's expensive."

His aunt's logic, as always, was unassailable. "She ski?"

"I wouldn't know. She was up early this morning—I think she's just a tourist. She mentioned she was going to take a walk down to the old burying ground."

Somehow, Julian thought, it figured.

SNOW HAD GOTTEN into her socks by the time Holly came to the far corner of the historic graveyard, where the thin, worn markers of perhaps a dozen Wingates rose from the drifts. Each stone seemed to lean in a different direction. She stared at the simple headstone of Abigail Wingate, who'd died at the age of three in 1838. It was for the memory of these Wingates, Holly thought, perhaps more than for herself or Grandpa Wingate or even future Wingates, that she wanted the Revere goblets back in the family.

"They were a sorry bunch," Julian Stiles said behind her.

Holly hadn't heard his approach in the snow and jumped, just managing to swallow a startled yell. "What do you think you're doing, sneaking up on me like that?"

"I wasn't sneaking. I just happened by."

She didn't believe that for a second. Julian Stiles "happened by" the way a lion "happened by" an innocent antelope. She said sourly, "You could have whistled or something."

"In a graveyard? How rude."

Yesterday she wouldn't have believed he'd concern himself with rudeness, but he did look the proper Yankee this morning. But for his vivid eyes, she might not have recognized him. His hair was combed, that Yankee jaw shaved, that taut, lean body free of plaster dust. He had on neatly pressed charcoal wool trousers, a preppy white shirt with button-down collar, a red foulard tie, a navy wool blazer and an unbuttoned Burberry overcoat. Yesterday's tattered outfit might have been just her imagination. The way things had been going so far, maybe it had been.

The man could not be figured, Holly thought. Tracking her down in a graveyard. She'd have to remain on her guard. Never let up. Expect Julian Danvers Stiles at every turn. She couldn't allow herself the luxury of thinking she had control over her situation in Millbrook. She needed to remember that Julian had friends and family here and she did not.

"When we were kids," Julian went on, "my brother and sister and I would sneak in here and play, but we'd catch hell if the pastor caught us."

"Did he?"

He flashed her a grin, unexpectedly warm—sexy. "Almost always."

"What kinds of things did you do in a graveyard?"

"Nothing malicious. Mostly we played cops and robbers, spies, orphans. You know, kid stuff."

Holly had seldom played any of those games, never orphan. It had cut too close to the bone. "Are your brother and sister younger or older?"

"Adam's three years older, Beth four years younger."

"You're the middle child, then."

"Caught between a rock and a hard place, I always say. What about you?"

"No brothers or sisters."

"Just you and your folks, huh?"

She shook her head. "Just me and my grandfather mostly."

He looked awkward, the way people did when they realized they'd made a painful assumption.

"Why were the Wingates such a sorry bunch?" Holly asked, as if searching for a bland change of subject.

Julian latched on to it. "I'm not an expert on Millbrook history, but I gather the Wingates weren't one of the luckiest—or most honest—families in the valley. They came to this area in the late eighteenth century and tried to hack a living out of the land, which isn't easy in these hills. They hung in there, though, until what's known around here as the Scandal of 1889."

"A scandal?" Holly manufactured a hungry-for-gossip look and even grinned. "Anything juicy?"

"You've been out here a while. Aren't you getting cold?"

She wondered how red her ears and nose were, but said, "Gossip always warms me up."

"This story's not gossip," Julian told her. "It's something that really happened."

"Maybe, but in my work, I've found there are often as many versions of an event as people interested in it— never mind people who actually were there or have a stake in what happened. And even eyewitnesses are notoriously unreliable."

He frowned. "Facts are facts."

"But how do you define a fact?"

"So what do you do, believe what you want?"

"Don't we all? Life isn't black-and-white. It's thousands of shades of gray."

"I suppose." Pausing, Julian used his boot as a mini-snowplow and began pushing out a circle of snow around him. He wasn't looking at Holly when, finally, he spoke. "By 1889, the Wingates were operating a sawmill up on the river outside of town. They were hardworking people, but there were tons of sawmills around here in those days, so competition was fairly tough. They just managed to get by."

"That's nothing to be ashamed of."

"I agree. After the Civil War, the board of directors of the Millbrook Preparatory Academy decided to offer a scholarship to one Vermont boy a year to attend what even then was considered one of the best schools in the country."

"For boys," Holly amended.

His foot stopped, and he nodded at her, his eyes so very green against the gloomy sky. "Right. You're sure you're not cold?"

"Not at all. This is fun."

"Standing in a graveyard talking about dead people?"

She laughed. "I guess it does sound ghoulish, but go on."

"To keep this short, Zachariah Wingate was granted a scholarship—the first boy from Millbrook who wasn't a Danvers or a Stiles to attend the academy. He lived at home and continued to help out at the sawmill, and although he wasn't immediately accepted by other students at the academy, he got decent grades and slowly won over his classmates. Then he made his mistake."

"What happened?"

"In his senior year, he decided he had the moral obligation to repay the academy for its generosity if he could. He presented the board of directors with a pair of sterling-silver goblets that had been made and signed by Paul Revere himself. He claimed Revere gave them to his great-grandfather after the Revolution, but that was disproven. In fact, he probably stole them from a collector. The long and short of it is, he was thrown out of school and his family was humiliated by the incident."

Holly felt the anger boiling inside her. More than a hundred years later and a Danvers-Stiles was still smearing the Wingate name! Believing their own version of what happened! Not giving poor Zachariah the slightest benefit of the doubt! But she said in a neutral voice, "How sad."

"For his family, yes. But Zachariah was a thief—"

"He was giving the goblets to the school. It's not as if he tried to keep them for himself."

"You know the saying: the road to hell is paved with good intentions."

Holly smiled tightly. "Was there any proof he'd stolen the goblets?"

"I wouldn't know, I wasn't there."

"What did Zachariah do after he was expelled from the academy?"

"Left town. His parents tried to hang on to the sawmill, but the scandal and Zachariah's absence hurt them. They ended up closing down. Within about five years there wasn't a Wingate left in Millbrook."

"You can hardly blame them."

There was more heat in her words than she'd intended, and Julian gave her a narrow-eyed look. She couldn't guess what he was thinking but imagined it wasn't anything positive.

"No, you can't," he said. "Scandal and gossip can be deadly in a small town."

Holly nodded and started pushing at the snow with her boots, the way he did, just to look a little less absorbed in his story of the hapless Wingates. "What happened to the goblets?"

"They disappeared with Zachariah."

"You think he took them?"

"I'm not sure what happened."

"Well, I guess it doesn't matter. *Now* I'm cold. Think I'll head back and have breakfast—"

"Yes, my aunt mentioned you were staying at the Windham House."

"You don't look too happy about that," Holly pointed out.

"I'm not."

"Did you tell her you don't believe my lost puppies story?"

He shook his head. "Not yet."

Holly found herself noticing how thick his lashes were, noticing the small scar near his left brow. Up close, his features weren't as regular nor as classically handsome as she'd have expected of a well-to-do Danvers-Stiles. Interesting, compelling, masculine—they were the words that came to her mind. She wished they hadn't. They indicated a physical awareness of him that she was madly trying to pretend she didn't feel. Matters were complicated enough as it was.

"Well, I wouldn't doubt me, if I were you," she told him. "I can be very convincing. I wouldn't want to put your aunt in the unhappy position of choosing between your word and mine."

He scowled. "Did you mention your crowbar to her?"

"No—"

"No one chases puppies with a crowbar."

"Lucky I had one along or I'd never have been able to follow the little rascals into a boarded-up house."

"They were never in the house."

She met his gaze dead-on. "I thought they were."

"Ms Paynter, there were no puppies."

She waved a green-gloved hand. "Who's to say? Look, you needn't worry."

"*I* needn't worry?"

"Not at all. You see, I have no intention of suing you."

"You don't." His voice was expressionless.

"No, no." Her tone was eminently reassuring. "How could I cause one of Millbrook's own the trouble and humiliation over such a lawsuit? I *could* sue, of course. A floor like that one up at the Danvers House is dangerous. As you yourself said, I could have been killed."

"It would have been your own damn fault—"

"Imagine the talk. A Millbrook Stiles's negligence causes the demise of an innocent woman from Houston who'd bravely risked her life to save a couple of stray puppies . . . My, my. The gossips would have fun with that for years."

"You're not funny."

"Funny? Mr. Stiles, I'm not trying to amuse you. I'm perfectly serious!"

"Sue me if you like. I'm not worried. You broke into the house, ignored the No Trespassing and Danger signs posted—and don't try to tell me you didn't see them. You went into that house at your own risk."

She sniffed. "Tell it to the judge. I still think I have a good case."

"Dammit, I refuse to get caught up in another one of your schemes. You're no more going to sue me than there were puppies out at the academy yesterday. You're just spinning me off into whatever direction you want me to go to save your own skin. And arguing only encourages you."

"Do you have a good lawyer?"

He ignored her. "I'll keep quiet about yesterday *only* for the time being and *only* because I have a feeling that a thief might crowbar her way into an abandoned house and run when she was caught, but she wouldn't show up at one of the nicest bed-and-breakfasts in town the same afternoon and wander around a graveyard the next morning. You present certain contradictions, Ms Paynter, that I intend to sort out."

"Do you? Well, have fun. When you find a couple of golden retriever puppies at that wreck of a house—"

"There were no damned golden retriever puppies," he said through clenched teeth.

"There might have been."

"And fun," he said, "is the last thing this is going to be."

With that, he stalked off through the snow. Holly watched him, wondering if a stoic Yankee like that would even know when he was having fun. But her job wasn't to analyze Julian Danvers Stiles, merely to set him straight about a certain pair of silver goblets.

She was cold and hungry and had had enough of old tombstones, but she headed back to the Windham House only after Julian Stiles's handsome figure was out of sight.

FELIX REICHMAN, a balding, portly expert in New England history, made himself comfortable on the couch in Julian's living room and examined the silver goblets through the thick lenses of his wire-framed glasses. He sighed, deeply impressed. "Paul Revere was an accomplished craftsman. Have you had these authenticated?"

"Yes," Julian said. It was early evening after a tiring day, complicated by one strawberry-haired Texan. The snowy graveyard had made her eyes seem even bluer. Less dishonest, perhaps, although he warned himself not to be fooled. He'd noticed the shape of her mouth, its softness, and had found himself wanting to make her smile. It was madness, he knew. Still, he wasn't one to deny his attraction to a woman—even a tale-telling trespasser.

"And insured?" Felix asked.

Julian forced himself to turn his attention to the matter at hand. Perhaps Reichman was only being thorough, but that was the second of two unnecessary questions that didn't deserve an answer. Julian objected to being underestimated—something he hoped he'd made clear to one Holly Paynter. Not that it made a damn bit of difference to her.

Sensing his mistake, the historian reddened. "Forgive me, I don't mean to question your judgment. It's just that . . . if you'll excuse me for saying so . . ." He paused, obviously debating whether to proceed, then blundered on, "Your security measures for protecting the goblets are . . . seem to be . . . ummm . . . nonexistent."

Julian laughed, and Reichman visibly relaxed. "I guess it must look that way. Felix, Millbrook is a small town. I've lived here most of my life. No one would steal the goblets. If anyone does, I'll know who."

"And you'll deal with the thief yourself?"

"Yes."

"I see." Felix cleared his throat, looking nervous again. "What about strangers?" he asked.

"I don't stay up nights worrying about strangers."

"Perhaps," Felix replied, "but Millbrook's become an attractive town for tourists and city people looking for a second home. I daresay you don't know everyone here the way you might have ten or fifteen years ago."

"Maybe not." Julian settled back in his leather reading chair next to the fire—his favorite spot. "Tourists would have to go out of their way to get to this part of Millbrook. They just don't come up here. I'd notice."

He wasn't bragging, simply stating what he considered obvious. His compact, rustic house was built into a hill overlooking a brook; its garage was at the end of a two-mile, single-lane dirt driveway. Even his own brother and sister griped about having to make the trip in to see him. He'd had to pay a fortune to get electricity out there and almost hadn't bothered. If he was going to be the town recluse, why not go whole hog and use candles and kerosene? He heated entirely with wood, and there wasn't a streetlight in miles. United Parcel Service and Federal Express left his packages at the sawmill where Mill Brook Post and Beam had its offices and equipment; he had a box at the post office for his mail. The occasional stranger that did stray his way got out of there, fast.

"What if you're not home to notice?" the persistent Reichman asked.

Smiling only slightly, Julian let his eyes drift to the two big mutts asleep on the warm stone hearth. They were mostly German shepherd. He had made the mistake of letting Abby and David, his niece and nephew, name them, which meant they went by the not-exactly-ferocious names of Penny and Inkspot. Pen and Ink for short. But they were just as suspicious of strangers as their master, and that was what counted.

Reichman still didn't give up. "A determined thief could shoot the dogs."

"Better than shooting Susannah Tibbet."

"The head teller at the bank?"

"None other. You want me to put the goblets in a safe-deposit box, right?"

"It would be wise."

"What's to stop a 'determined thief' from shooting his way into a bank?"

"Banks are equipped—"

"I know. But I'll keep the goblets here. I don't own anything that means more to me than living the kind of life I want to live. I'm not inviting a thief, but I'm not going to be paranoid about one, either. Until the restaurant opens and I put them on display there, the goblets will be fine right here on my mantel. If not, to hell with them."

Reichman paled a bit at his new client's cavalier attitude, but he nodded. "As you wish."

Julian nodded back, but was silent. Security wasn't Felix Reichman's concern and they both knew it. Explaining had been a courtesy on Julian's part. He understood that a pair of sterling-silver goblets as beautiful as these, and shrouded in such mystery, meant more to a man like Felix than they did to most people. If stolen, he would mourn their loss more than their new owner would.

"The publicity might invite thieves," Julian said, "but I don't think so. Millbrook's a bit off the beaten track, you might say. Now. About your job. Do you understand what I'm after?"

"I think so. You want a history of the goblets. I'll substantiate the facts as best I can—"

"Don't be afraid to report rumors and suppositions, only mark them as such."

Felix smiled indulgently. "Now you're venturing into my territory."

Julian agreed. During the summer, Reichman, a retired professor, operated a rare and used bookstore, but he closed up for the winter and did research for people, mostly writers and academics. Never for someone like Julian Stiles. He'd told Julian as much. But Felix was taking the job; the goblets and the mystery surrounding them had piqued his interest—and he and Dorothy Windham were friends. For those reasons, he'd tolerate her nephew.

They discussed the specifics of the research assignment. Julian couldn't help wondering what the officious, portly gentleman would say when he discovered most of what he reported would end up on a restaurant menu.

"I'm not sure how long this will take," Felix said. "Do you need the research completed by any special date?"

"No. Take your time."

Thanking Julian, Felix left, and Julian watched from the window as his guest departed. Since his retirement, the historian had adopted all the trappings of a rural life-style. He had the requisite ski jacket, the tough boots, the worn wool sweater, the catalog trousers and chamois shirt. But somehow Julian was surprised to see the urbane intellectual bouncing down his frozen driveway in a mud-splattered, four-wheel-drive Jeep.

When the sound faded into the distance and then altogether, Julian was struck by the silence of his house. He could hear the dogs breathing and the crackle of the fire, and he closed his eyes a moment, enjoying the peace. It was one of the aspects he most loved about his isolated existence. And, at times, most hated.

Finally he returned the goblets to the iron case in which he'd found them buried in the old dirt cellar of the Danvers House. He'd had the goblets polished and the case cleaned and lined with fresh black velvet. They were in remarkable condition. He enjoyed brushing his fingertips across the silver, smooth and cool to the touch. But he wasn't a man to let any material possession change his life.

And yet . . .

He shut the case hard, and the dogs stirred behind him. They seemed to sense his uneasiness. There was something about the goblets he didn't understand. He hoped Felix Reichman's history would explain why a strange feeling overcame him whenever he handled the damned things. He sensed, oddly and uncontrollably, that they had the capacity to change his life. Last night, there had seemed such an air of inevitability about it that he'd almost marched down to the house and re-buried them. But that was too extreme, and he wasn't a coward. He was a thorough man, however. He had to know what the goblets meant.

He would wait for Felix's report.

Meanwhile, he would entertain himself with finding out what had brought Holly Paynter to Millbrook. The goblets, perhaps? It was farfetched, but not beyond the realm of possibility. He settled back in his chair and closed his eyes, imagining her stealing to his house in the dead of night to steal the Revere goblets.

Come ahead, sweetheart, he thought. Come ahead.

3

"THE BASTARD might as well live on the moon," Holly grumbled, tucking her recently purchased map of Millbrook back into the glove compartment of her van. She sat back with a sigh. So far her third day in Millbrook wasn't going any better then her first and second, but she did feel better that at least she'd discovered where Julian Stiles lived, for future reference. All she'd had to do was explain to the man at the gas station where she'd bought her town map that she'd stumbled on a stray golden retriever pup with tags declaring Julian Stiles as the owner, and he'd graciously pointed out Julian's house.

"Lives out in the woods a piece," the man had said. His greasy nametag identified him as Bert. "Driveway's two, two-and-a-half miles long. Not many folks like to drive it this time of year, but Julian doesn't seem to mind."

"Is he a hermit or what?" Holly had asked.

"Just keeps to himself is all."

That was the only good news she'd had since crossing the Millbrook town line the day before yesterday. If Julian kept to himself, he wouldn't necessarily find out she'd been buying maps and having his place redmarked for her. Not that she especially cared if he found out. She was hell to intimidate, and rattling Julian

Danvers Stiles could suit her purposes. Maybe he'd make a mistake or just give her the goblets to get her out of town.

"Didn't know he had a puppy," the man at the gas station had said, perplexed. "He's already got two dogs. What's he want with another?"

"Beats me. Are the other two goldens?"

"German shepherd."

Given her healthy dose of Wingate bad luck, it figured.

She supposed she could march down to a lawyer's office, explain she was Zachariah Wingate's great-granddaughter and wanted her family's goblets back. The powers-that-were at the Millbrook Preparatory Academy back in 1889—namely Jonathan Stiles and Edward Danvers—had rejected them, hadn't they? They'd never *proven* Zachariah had stolen them, had they? All Holly had to do was let her and Julian's lawyers fight it out in court.

But where was the challenge in that? She'd rather stand up for what was right and restore the goblets to the Wingates, then slip back to Florida and finish her wanderings there before going home to Houston for a few weeks. She wasn't one to stay anywhere for long.

Unlike Julian Stiles. Obviously he was a stick-in-the-mud of the first order. What did he do out there in the middle of nowhere when it snowed?

Pushing Julian from her mind, she followed the Mill Brook up into the hills beyond Old Millbrook Common. She had spent most of the morning poking around town, stopping at the library to surreptitiously look up the Wingates. She'd learned the old Wingate sawmill was located farther up the river, and although she had no idea if it remained standing, she was determined at least to see the site where her ancestors had made their hard-scrabble living.

There was no need to rush to get the goblets back. It was an inconvenience that Julian had caught her sneaking around in the Danvers House and out among the Wingate stones in the Old Millbrook Burying Ground—*and* had her license number and was related to the owner of the bed-and-breakfast where she was staying. But she'd have to work around all that. She wasn't leaving town without the goblets. Julian might have an idea of who to come looking for when they turned up missing, but she couldn't worry about that now. From here on out, she'd be careful and just bide her time.

With residential Millbrook well behind her, in a few minutes she came to a low-slung building of dark, rough-cut lumber with a steeply pitched slate roof and a stone foundation. It was nestled into a hillside along a rapidly flowing section of the river. A small gravel parking lot was carved into the hill, below an old dam and its small mill pond. Move the Land Rover, Ford truck and beat-up old Chevy out of the way, Holly thought, and the place was worthy of the front of a picture postcard.

Holly started to turn into the parking lot.

Then she spotted the small hand-hewn sign posted out front: Millbrook Post and Beam.

"How quaint," she muttered, wondering if she should turn back. "Oh, what the hell."

But it did stand to reason a Danvers-Stiles would have profited from a Wingate's misfortunes, didn't it?

She pulled in next to the Land Rover. The air was colder up in the hills, close to the water, but Holly didn't mind. Maybe a good gust of cold air would restore her equilibrium. The Wingate sawmill being in the hands of the descendants of Jonathan Stiles and Edward Danvers didn't sit too well with her. *What next?* She felt frayed on the edges, ready to short-circuit.

The stone steps leading to the upper main floor of the old sawmill were slippery, but there was a rail and Holly managed. She followed the flagstone walk to the front door, which was made of the same solid rough-cut lumber as the exterior. A small plaque told her to please come in. She did.

The main floor of Mill Brook Post and Beam was offices, a large, open room divided into a half-dozen work spaces. The walls and floors were of old, rough, dark board, but paned windows offered stunning views of the river and mill pond, as well as much needed sunlight.

Standing in the space that served as an entry, their mittens dripping onto a thick straw mat, were a girl of about eleven and a boy a few years younger. They looked contrite as a man, green-eyed and powerfully built, older than Julian, quietly dressed them down.

"You're not to go near the saws unless I'm with you," he told them. "You both know that."

They nodded. Obviously they did know.

"There are no second chances with saws."

This time they didn't nod, although Holly guessed they knew that as well. The man—Julian's brother Adam?—was missing his left hand.

"We're sorry," the girl said.

"Sorry doesn't get it, Abby. I believe in actions, not words."

"Fred was with us—"

"Fred isn't your dad, is he?" His eyes narrowed, and his voice lowered even more. "Stay away from the saws."

Holly could see the children swallow. She was swallowing herself. Like Julian, this Stiles wasn't one to cross. Then all at once the outraged father's face relaxed, and he gave something that passed for a smile as he patted his children's cheeks. "Go warm up by the wood stove. Then get busy. The steps outside and the parking lot need sanding."

They grinned brightly, and the boy said, "Will you pay us?"

"No, I'm not going to pay you! I'll spare you a hide-tanning is what I'll do."

Something about his tone and look of unconditional love toward his children made Holly doubt he'd ever laid a hand on either one of them. He came forward to greet her. About Julian's height, he wore heavy corduroys, a functional plaid wool shirt and scarred boots. "Hi, I'm Adam Stiles," he said. "What can I do for you?"

She didn't want to be too obvious about looking around for Julian, so she simply answered him in a straightforward manner. "My name's Holly Paynter.

I'm staying here in town and just thought I'd come have a look at the mill."

"Great. I'll get someone to show you around."

"Allow me," Julian said, coming forward. He was dressed like a mountain man again today, yesterday's preppy tie and blazer a sudden incongruity. If she presented certain contradictions, so did he.

Holly dealt with, Adam retreated to his work area before she could voice a decent protest. For once, she was at a loss for words. She realized she should have turned around and headed back to town the moment she'd discovered the old Wingate sawmill was in enemy hands.

"Hello, there," Julian said cheerfully.

"Hi. I was just poking around town and couldn't resist stopping by."

"You weren't lured here by lost puppies?"

She smiled. "Nope."

"Come on. As long as you're here, I'll give you the nickel tour. Know anything about Mill Brook Post and Beam?"

"Not really."

"We sell high-quality kits for houses and other buildings. We cut most of the wood right here ourselves, using native trees. Post and beam structures go up fast. They're versatile, economical, attractive. Anyway, we're doing all right."

"That's nice," Holly said, hoping she'd kept the acid out of her tone. Didn't his people *always* fare well? "It's a family business?"

"Right. My mother's family has owned the mill since the turn of the century, but it's only been in the last ten years or so that we've really made it pay—once we got into the post-and-beam-kit business. Adam pretty much runs the sawmill side of things and works directly with clients, helping them choose the best building designs for their needs and sites. Beth does some of that as well, but her main responsibilities are advertisement and promotion, mailing lists, keeping people paid and coming to work. We've got the business worked out so any one of us can handle the other's job. Adam, Beth and I all know how to run every piece of equipment in the place. We're all needed, but none of us is essential to keep the place running."

"Then you get along pretty well?"

"Sure. We have our squabbles, but we try to make most decisions on a consensus basis."

"What about your parents?"

"They're retired. At the moment they're vacationing in Florida."

"Smart people," Holly muttered.

He led her down a narrow set of stairs, explaining that they were in the original early nineteenth-century structure, with its waterwheel and old up-and-down saw, still in use. It was one of the few water-powered sawmills left in New England. There was also a newer mill, using modern equipment, out back.

"Sorry about that little scene you wandered into," Julian said. "Abby and David tend to be somewhat overconfident of their ability to fend for themselves around here."

"You don't have to apologize."

She meant it: the saws were frighteningly huge. Holly could understand why Adam Stiles didn't want his children running around down here unescorted.

"The way Adam works, this is their home away from home."

"Does their mother work here as well?"

Julian's face tightened, and instantly Holly realized she'd brought up a difficult subject. She tried to back out gracefully, but Julian shook off her halfhearted attempt. She was, she had to admit, madly curious.

"Adam's wife was killed in a car accident four years ago," Julian explained. "Three months later he lost his left hand in a saw accident. It was a rough period—for all of us."

Holly wondered what that meant, but decided it wasn't her place to press for specifics. "I'm sorry."

"Don't tell Adam that—he hates sympathy. He rides herd on all of us, but that's just his way. We all know he's not half as indispensable as he thinks he is. And he's got the kids. They have a way of keeping him from turning into a total curmudgeon."

And what, she wondered, *stops you?* She wondered why he lived out in the woods all alone, how he could stand the isolation. She liked being on the road, poking around here and there, snooping for story ideas. Being in one place for too long drove her nuts.

With the smell of sawdust all around them, Julian showed her around and explained about logs and saws and the central concept behind post and beam, how all load-bearing walls were on the exterior, making for an infinitely maleable interior. Holly didn't have to feign interest. She'd always been an informational sponge.

Back upstairs, he loaded her up with brochures and booklets illustrating various basic house plans.

"Daydream material," she said, thanking him.

"You don't have a house, then?"

She could see the reluctant interest in his eyes; he wanted to know more about her. "Just an apartment in Houston, but I live out of my van a lot."

"What do you do for a living?"

"Tell stories," she said, with a grin.

He gave her a skeptical, "Right," and warned her to watch for icy patches on her way out.

Holly could take a hint as well as anyone, when it suited her. "Thanks for your time—and I'll be careful."

"Good. I'd hate to have to scrape you off the steps."

There was a sudden husky, sensual quality to his voice that made the blood rush to her cheeks. She'd hate to have him scrape her off the steps as well. And injury had damned little to do with her uneasiness. She made her way outside and held tight to the handrail, imagining Julian Stiles sweeping her up into his arms after she'd fallen, pressing her against his warm, solid chest.

"Lordy," she muttered to herself.

The image, however, didn't disappear of its own volition. She had to force it back to her subconscious. She was far, far too drawn to Julian Stiles. To his rare smiles, to his tenacity, to his strong legs and shoulders. To the questions and contradictions he presented. She wanted to know him better. *In spite of his being a Danvers-Stiles, or because of it?*

Letting the question linger, unanswered, she climbed back into her van. When, she wondered, was he going to put her illicit presence in the Danvers House, her poking around the Old Millbrook Burying Ground and her interest in the sawmill together and come up with the Paul Revere goblets?

Knowing Julian Danvers Stiles as she was beginning to know him, she'd bet it'd be sooner rather than later.

"And then what?" she asked herself aloud.

She'd just have to punt.

"WAS THAT WHO I think it was?" Beth Stiles asked, coming in from the storage room.

Julian frowned at his sister. One could never be entirely sure what she was getting at. She was a solidly built woman with the Danvers' tawny hair and the Stiles green eyes, the exact shade of his own. She had married right out of college, divorced three miserable years later, then wandered around for a few years before coming home, finally, to Millbrook. She prided herself on being able to do anything her two older brothers could do. Julian, for one, had learned not to doubt her. His equal in the corporation, Beth was vital to the success of Mill Brook Post and Beam.

"You mean the redhead who just left?" he asked, just to be sure.

"Yeah. Holly Paynter, right?"

Julian nodded. "I take it you've been down to Aunt Doe's."

"No, but she told me about her. It's pretty exciting she's picked Millbrook to investigate. I don't think she's ever done anything set in New England."

"Beth, what are you talking about?"

"Holly Paynter," she said, as if that should clear up everything. She sighed. "You've never heard of her?"

"No. Should I have?"

"Knowing you, probably not. She's a storyteller."

Julian couldn't argue with that.

"She's performed all over the world," Beth went on eagerly. "She's done live performances, radio, television. I read somewhere she once did a birthday party for a European princess. I always thought storytellers would be a little too brown rice and granola for me, but I heard her on the radio once, and she's real straightforward and down-to-earth—and absolutely captivating. She got me caught up in her story. She made it seem so natural, effortless."

She was good, he thought. If he hadn't seen the one set of tracks across the academy football field, Julian might have swallowed her puppy story himself. How clever of her to find a way to make a living putting that glib tongue of hers to work.

"Why do you think she's so interested in Millbrook?" he asked.

"Who knows? I just think it's neat that she is."

His sister's enthusiasm for Holly Paynter was getting on Julian's nerves. If she was so damned reputable, how come she hadn't come clean to him by now? Why the lost puppies? Why'd she been snooping around in the Danvers House? He could have had her arrested. She'd risked her reputation with her crowbar and lies.

Had he misjudged her?

Beth's evidence to the contrary, he didn't think so—at least not entirely. He'd looked into those lying blue eyes and he'd seen trouble.

He decided to head into town.

The local bookstore had two copies of a collection of tales of the American Southwest written by Holly Paynter. Her picture—lying eyes and all—was on the back cover. He paid twenty dollars for a copy. The couple who ran the bookstore asked him if he realized Holly Paynter was in town.

"I just heard," he said dryly. There were no secrets in a small town, he remembered. He wondered if Ms. Paynter realized that.

"We also have one of her cassettes," Mrs. Stoka pointed out.

Julian bought one of those as well.

He walked down to the Danvers Memorial Library and looked up Holly Paynter in the *Reader's Guide to Periodical Literature.* She'd been mentioned in a *Newsweek* article on storytellers a few months back. He tracked it down, made a photocopy and tucked it inside his bookstore bag.

His reading and listening material for the evening set, he tossed the lot into the back of his Land Rover. By nightfall he'd know more about the strawberry-haired, crowbar-toting, lying-eyed woman from Texas than he did right now. But he had a feeling it wouldn't be anywhere near enough.

"You're hooked," he said to himself, and started back up to the sawmill, stopping for gas along the way.

Bert told him about the map he'd sold Holly Paynter and asked about his missing golden retriever, mumbling something about what the devil he'd want with another damned dog.

"You pointed out my place to her?" he asked, just to make sure.

"Yep. Wouldn't want anyone getting lost up there."

"I wouldn't, either. Thanks, Bert."

Yes, he thought, wasn't Holly Paynter the sweetest, most talented storyteller? Wasn't it just Millbrook's great fortune to have her snooping around town?

The lady was up to something, and he'd have to be a damned idiot not to realize what.

She was after his Paul Revere sterling-silver goblets.

He supposed they'd make a good story. So why not ask him to see them? Why all the secrecy?

What was her game?

He got as far as Old Millbrook Common. It was tea-time at the Windham House, and Holly's beat-up van was parked outside. He wasn't sure confronting her before he'd done his homework on her was the smart-est idea. But what the hell. Things had been quiet at the mill today, and Aunt Doe always appreciated having one of her nieces or nephews drop in.

A HOT BATH after her ordeal at the sawmill had revived Holly. She was confident once more she could handle whatever Julian had a mind to throw at her. The man was a difficult audience. He wasn't one to "willingly suspend disbelief" without a struggle. Probably was the type who sat up nights reading car magazines and home-repair manuals instead of a good, juicy novel. A man with both feet flat on the floor at all times.

She wondered what he did for fun. Rescue worthless old buildings from the wrecking crane? Keep a valu-able family heirloom from its rightful owner? What hi-larity.

Suspicious-natured individual that he was, if he started putting this and that together he could easily come up with a prospective thief of "his" Revere goblets. She didn't want that. He was territorial enough without giving him good reason to be.

"Will you just stop thinking about that man!" she growled aloud to herself.

But she couldn't. She'd been trying, it seemed, ever since she'd crashed through his ceiling.

She got out her all-purpose sapphire-blue knit dress, unrolled it, gave it a shake and put it on. She could dress it up, dress it down, add a scarf, add her best gold jewelry, wear it with boots or wear it with flats. Any wrinkles would hang out in minutes. The perfect traveling dress. She decided on a scarf, which she tied at a rather rakish angle, then stuck gold posts in her ears, fluffed up her hair with her fingers, dabbed on some lipstick and a little mascara and looked in the bathroom mirror.

"Lordy," she said to her reflection. "You're looking more and more like a Yankee every minute you're here."

She slipped into her black flats and headed downstairs.

Dorothy Windham had set up for tea in an elegant alcove overlooking the backyard and bird feeders. An oval Queen Anne table was set with a silver tray of tiny muffins and scones, slices of cheese and pots of jam and whipped butter. There were just two cups and saucers—a relief. Holly's brain was too unsettled to cope with a crowd. She hoped it would be just her and her hostess.

Such was not her luck.

Julian came into the little parlor, a scarred leather jacket over his flannel shirt and corduroys. He was carrying a porcelain teapot. "Madam," he said in a mock snooty accent, "tea is served."

"Where did you come from?"

"Just happened by."

His favorite line, obviously. She scowled. "What about your aunt?"

"Called away at the last minute. It seems someone found a couple of stray golden retriever puppies up at the academy. Aunt Doe's such a soft touch. She's gone to help get them to the vet."

"You're lying," she said, seating herself on the Duncan Phyfe sofa.

"You should know."

He filled the two cups with tea and sat on the other end of the sofa. He could have chosen one of the wing chairs, but didn't. Holly forced herself not to scoot down even farther. She was finished being cocky, she thought. She'd talked herself into believing she could march into Millbrook, Vermont on her own terms. Pure, unadulterated cockiness. She was a *Wingate*. She was going to have to keep her eyes open, anticipate the worst, be ready for it—and never, never allow herself to be lured into thinking luck was with her. It seldom was, and it certainly wouldn't be here.

Hard work and craftiness. They were what she'd always relied on. Never on luck.

Taking her cup and saucer in hand, she got herself back under control after the shock of having Julian Stiles turn up again. She prided herself on not being a fidgeter. Grandpa Wingate had never tolerated fidgeting. "You need to sit, sit," he used to say. "You need to walk, walk. Just don't fidget. It's a waste of good energy."

Grandpa had never been one to waste anything. His teachings on that subject had helped Holly first to be aware of unconscious movements and expressions, and then to learn to control them. It was an ability that came in handy in her storytelling. To truly captivate an audience, she had to be conscious of every part of her body, not just what came out of her mouth.

She couldn't fidget.

With Julian's vibrant gaze on her, however, she caught herself shaking an ankle, then biting the insides of her cheeks, then twisting her fingers together.

Fidgeting.

And wondering what it would take to captivate *him*.

Aggravated, she put a stop to all unnecessary movements and intrusive thoughts. The tea was very hot and soothing. It helped calm her.

"Do you come by here often for tea?" she asked.

"No."

She wasn't one to beat around the bush, either. "Then you're here because you're keeping an eye on me."

He leaned back. "You could say that."

His expression was calculating and observant, the wolf figuring out how he could have *both* Little Red Riding-Hood and her grandmother for his dinner. Holly reminded herself Little Red Riding-Hood had won in the end. She'd had help from the woodcutter, but Holly was used to depending on herself. And unlike the fairy-tale character, she knew not to trust wolves, no matter how charming.

And especially when they were part Danvers *and* part Stiles.

"Why didn't you tell me you're a storyteller?" Julian asked.

Holly tried to conceal her surprise; a storyteller was part actress. "How did you find out?"

"My sister, Beth, and half the town, it seems, recognized your name."

"Oh." Sometimes she forgot that people knew her from her work.

"The consensus is you're here investigating story possibilities."

"Not just on vacation?"

"I'd say not." He held his teacup close to his mouth, but wasn't drinking, just watching her. The delicate porcelain looked incongruous and yet curiously right in his big hand. Holly noticed his calluses, his clipped, spotlessly clean nails. "There's a difference, isn't there, between a story and an outright lie?"

"Usually."

"Don't you ever give a straight answer?"

"I don't necessarily give easy answers, if that's what you want. Truth is often in the eye of the beholder."

"Fair enough. What's it like being a storyteller?"

"Like anything else, it has its costs, its rewards, its sacrifices. Some stories come easily, but are hard to tell. With others, it's vice versa. Then there are those that don't come easily and aren't easy to tell, but they're worth the extra trouble. I guess some are easy all the way around, but not many. There's a great deal of hard work and frustration involved with establishing a career in storytelling, in just making ends meet."

"You travel a lot?"

"Between performances and research, I'm on the road more often than not."

"Hard life," he said. "What specifically brings you to Millbrook?"

She didn't trust his tone of voice. *What's he know?* The man was thorough, tenacious, self-possessed. Of course, so was she. Whatever he'd guessed, she'd just have to outbrazen him.

"The Wingates," she said.

He sat back, obviously thinking he'd succeeded in *forcing* her to admit something. "I see."

"I was planning a trip to Vermont in wintertime anyway, but I'd hoped to come a little later in the season—around maple-sugaring time."

"That's spring," he pointed out.

"All in the eye of the beholder." She set her tea back on the table and reached for a scone, leaving it unbuttered but adding just a dollop of spiced peach preserves. She could feel Julian's unrelenting gaze on her. "Anyway, I was sitting on a bench behind Cinderella's Castle at Disney World, just enjoying the mob scene, when I spotted the wire-service piece on your discovery of the goblets. It sparked my storyteller's curiosity. So I hopped in my van and headed north."

"It's that simple?"

"Yes."

"Then why not tell me sooner?"

She shrugged. "I prefer to maintain a low profile when I'm investigating a story possibility. Frankly I had no idea anyone in Millbrook would have heard of me. I've never performed in Vermont."

He, too, returned his tea to the table, then leaned over toward her. She could smell his tangy cologne and see the tiny scar at the corner of his left eyebrow. Her fingers tingled at the thought of touching him. *This is becoming a nasty business*, she thought. She wanted to dismiss Julian Danvers Stiles as an uncomplicated, hateful descendant of the two men that had abused her great-grandfather in the last century. As the unthinking, uncaring contemporary Danvers-Stiles who didn't give a damn who the Revere goblets really belonged to. She wanted to hang on to all her presuppositions, do what she came to do and leave Millbrook without a whiff of regret.

That was becoming an increasingly elusive goal.

Then he said darkly, "Lady, don't play games with me."

She had to fight a smile. *Go ahead and make this easier on me*. "Lady," she replied coolly, "is the name of a cocker spaniel."

He sighed, sitting back a moment. His eyes seemed to be searching hers. "I surrender," he said, and rose abruptly. "For now."

"Am I supposed to feel intimidated?"

"Only if you're up to no-good."

It was his parting shot. Remaining seated, Holly watched him stalk out into the hall. As hard as she looked, she couldn't detect a hint of surrender in his walk. His back, his powerful shoulders, his long legs— they all registered confidence and self-assurance.

Suddenly she wished she hadn't done anything so precipitous as rousing Julian Stiles to the chase. But she'd never been one to whimper over what she couldn't change: self-pity wasn't her style.

And, she had to admit, if only to herself, the prospect of having that strong-backed Yankee on her tail did have its points. There was the challenge, of course—she did love a challenge—but there was also the simple fact that she was intrigued by the guy. What made Julian Danvers Stiles tick?

She wanted to know, she decided, and trying—vainly—to blame such idiocy on her storyteller's curiosity and not any attraction to him on her part, she poured herself another cup of tea.

4

THAT EVENING, Julian settled into his comfortable chair near the fire, Pen's head resting against one foot, and methodically went through his material on the storyteller from Texas. He read every word of her book of tales and the photocopied article. He even took notes. It was a way, he knew, of trying to distance himself, but he had already discovered that maintaining objectivity when Holly Paynter was around was impossible.

Tea had nearly done him in. Even now, as he stared into the fire, he could see the fit of her dress over her slender body, the swell of her soft breasts. The sapphire knit had matched the blue of her tantalizing eyes. Even covered head to toe in plaster dust she'd been damned difficult to resist. He'd found himself wanting to smile at her, laugh with her. Wanting to touch the corner of her mouth with his thumb...his lips, his tongue.

Of course, he told himself, that was an element of her challenge. He wasn't going to underestimate her. She had been just as aware of the sensual undercurrents between them as he was.

What kind of stories, he wondered, would she tell in bed?

With a growl of pure frustration, he took the dogs outside for a while, walking through the snow, just them and the wind for company. It was after midnight, and he was bleary-eyed and stiff from poring over Holly Paynter's words and profile, thinking about her. The sky was clearing, the clouds pushing off to the east, and the stars and sliver of a moon were glittering in the blackness to the west.

He found himself wishing he wasn't alone. It wasn't always like that; he enjoyed his solitude. But tonight was different. He'd have liked to point out stars with someone—a woman, he thought. They could hold hands, get cold together. Afterward they could go inside and warm up by the fire, making love.

And he could still see Holly studying him from the opposite end of the couch over tea. Trying to calculate how much he knew. Trying to keep her own attraction to him at bay. She was so damned lively and energetic, so quick-witted, so relentless.

"God, man, what are you doing to yourself?" he muttered, and called the dogs, heading inside. It was time to get back to work.

The brisk air had given him a second wind, and he popped her cassette into his tape player. Her voice filled the small room, enveloping him, instantly pulling him under her spell. He closed his eyes, willingly transported into the world she created for her listeners, seemingly without effort.

At the end, he realized he hadn't taken down a single note or done anything except sit there like a damned lump and listen. Annoyed with himself, he rewound the tape and listened again, notebook in hand, and jotted down any names, dates, places, possible clues as to why she had come all the way to Millbrook, Vermont, after a couple of Paul Revere sterling-silver goblets. Just because they might make a good story? Given her abilities and obvious devotion to her craft, he supposed it was possible. But he didn't believe it. There had to be another reason—a deeper motive, as they said in storyteller talk.

He took her book and trudged up to his loft bedroom. He couldn't remember feeling so tired, and he'd hardly done a lick of physical labor all day. What in hell was wrong with him? He sighed, aggravated and kicked off his boots, falling into bed with his clothes on and staring at the exposed beam-and-wood ceiling. Then he flipped on his bed-stand light, and once more opened Holly Paynter's book, beginning with the title page. He must have missed *something*.

He had.

Dropping his stockinged feet to the floor, Julian sat up straight. By God, there it was.

The book was copyrighted in the name of Holly Wingate Paynter.

Wingate.

"I'll be damned."

He glanced at the clock. It was 2:00 a.m. Too late to head into town and roust the blue-eyed Texan out of her cozy bed. He wasn't worried about disturbing her. She was going to be plenty disturbed when he got hold of her! He wanted some answers. But they'd have to wait, because he wasn't going to go pounding on his aunt's door in the middle of the night and get her all worried.

Maybe Felix Reichman would know something by now. He looked like the night-owl type.

Julian grabbed the phone and dialed.

Felix answered on the second ring. Julian apologized for the late call, but Felix assured him it was no problem. "I love to listen to opera on winter nights, especially after midnight."

"Is that what I hear warbling in the background?"

"That's the last act of *Madame Butterfly.* Just a moment, I'll turn it down."

The man, Julian thought, was an eccentric.

Felix was back in a few seconds. "There. What can I do for you?"

"Well." Suddenly Julian felt like an idiot. "I know you've only just gotten started, but in your research into the goblets, have you come across any indication that Zachariah Wingate might not have stolen them after all?"

"Nothing specific, no. But I haven't discovered anything that would confirm that he *did* steal them. It seems to be a case of his word against that of the headmaster and the chairman of the academy's board of directors."

Edward Danvers and Jonathan Stiles. The two families had intermarried after the scandal, in 1900, when Jonathan's daughter married Edward's great-nephew. Zachariah Wingate was long gone by then, to where no one knew—or particularly cared.

Julian leaned back against his headboard. "I need proof, one way or the other."

"I'll see what I can find out, but I must warn you. It's been over a hundred years. There may be no way to prove either side."

"Fair enough. Stay on the case, Felix. And thanks."

As he hung up, Julian could hear *Madame Butterfly* moving toward its tragic, inevitable conclusion. *In twenty years,* he wondered, *will I, too, be home alone listening to sad operas so late at night?*

HOLLY FELT A BIT LIKE Little Red Riding-Hood taking the shortcut through the forbidden forest late the next morning as she bumped along what had to be the road to nowhere. It was narrow, unpaved, winding, hilly, covered with packed snow and dotted with patches of ice that appeared without warning. Either she'd end up in a ditch or she'd survive this ordeal.

"What ditch?" she grumbled to herself.

There were no ditches, no shoulders, no guardrails to the one-lane driveway. It was just a strip carved out of the forest, which seemed to be working hard to reclaim its land. Snow-laden evergreen branches hung low over the road. Giant boulders loomed on its edge. A shallow swamp—wetland, in contemporary parlance—had seeped beyond its boundaries, creating a thick, treacherous patch of ice that Julian, and therefore Holly, had to go around.

Yet when she dared to take her eyes off the road, just for an instant, she could see the sparkling beauty of the landscape and feel its peace . . . and was captivated. Yesterday's clouds had pushed on to the east. In their place was a high, cloudless blue sky with a sun so bright that it glittered on the newly fallen white, white snow, hurting her eyes.

"Why don't you meet me for lunch," Julian had suggested in a surprising nine-o'clock call.

The invitation sounded suspicious to her. She told him so.

He laughed, apparently not taking offense. "I thought you might like a look at the Revere goblets I found."

"Well, I would, of course, but only if it's no trouble. I don't have to see them—" *Just swipe 'em and go.*

"It's no trouble. Is noon all right?"

"Fine. Um . . . where's your house?"

"Ask Bert at the gas station," he said, hanging up.

Her van, a true workhorse, negotiated a tight, treacherous S-curve that had her pulse racing by the time she'd twisted out of it. How could anyone actually live out here? she wondered.

At last the woods opened into a clearing and the driveway widened slightly—and there was a house. Civilization! A Land Rover was parked in front of the garage door; Holly eased in behind it. She peeled her fingers off the steering wheel, took a breath and decided her knees weren't so wobbly they'd fold up underneath her when she got out of the van.

Two enormous dogs scrambled out from under a low-hanging evergreen, barking and carrying on until their master emerged from the house and hollered something they, but not Holly, could understand. The creatures backed off.

"Meet Pen and Ink," Julian said, looking reassuringly calm. He was in jeans, a long-sleeved T-shirt and old mud boots, but he looked so damnably sexy Holly could feel her cheeks grow hot and her fingertips tingle. Madness!

She greeted the dogs cautiously.

Julian added, "They're not as ferocious as they think they are, but they do keep an eye on the place."

"Not good with strangers, are they?"

He smiled nastily. "Like their master."

Holly decided that was a point to remember, should she need to double back alone to restore the goblets to their rightful place in the Wingate family. Luckily she wasn't afraid of dogs, and if in the short time she was here this afternoon she made friends with them...well, she wouldn't be a stranger, would she?

Julian was eyeing her from the gravel walk. "How'd you make out getting here?"

"I thought you might end up having to fish me out of the swamp a couple of times, but I managed. I never really lost control of my van. How long is that driveway?"

"Two-point-three miles."

"It feels like thirty."

"Maybe," he said, pushing open the solid wood door, "but I think the trip's worth the price."

Holly wasn't so sure. The isolated setting of the house had a certain spectacular beauty, with the clearing giving way to a steep, wooded hillside. She could just imagine the dramatic views from inside the house. At the bottom of the hill flowed a winding stream. In the silence, she could hear the clear, icy water rushing over the rocks. Very nice, very soothing. But what about people?

Since she was still planning to restore the goblets to the Wingate family—Julian would say steal them— Holly decided to be polite. "It's a lovely spot. How far's your nearest neighbor?"

"Oh, miles."

She'd know exactly how many miles, have phone numbers posted and people to check in on her regularly to make sure she hadn't broken a leg or something out there in the boonies.

She followed him into the small, rustic house, straight into an efficient galley kitchen. Other than a dirty coffee mug in the sink, it was spotlessly clean. Holly tried to imagine Julian Stiles scrubbing his own refrigerator and found, to her surprise, that she could. He wasn't a man who shied away from physical labor. The vice president of Mill Brook Post and Beam she'd imagined on her way up from Florida would have hired someone to do the job for him, assumed it was "woman's work" or simply not bothered.

"What about when it snows?" she asked. "Do you have to plow your own driveway?"

"Since it's not a town road, yes. I don't mind. I've got a four-wheel-drive truck with a plow, and I can hook a plow on to the Rover if I need to. Being so far out, I keep two vehicles on the road. In case one gives out, I've always got the other. There are adjustments to make to live this kind of life," he added, "but not as many as you might think."

"Feels like the back end of nowhere to me."

He laughed. "There're times I'd agree with you, mostly at about ten o'clock at night when I'm dying for a pizza or Chinese food."

"I'm partial to take-out Tex-Mex myself."

"I've learned to keep a well-stocked fridge. Speaking of which—can I get you anything?"

"No, thanks."

Holly found herself less anxious to get on with the business of the goblets than she'd expected, more willing to hear about Julian's life out here in the wilderness. It was a storyteller's need to know, she told herself. But leaning against the refrigerator, she watched him wash his hands with a mean-looking bar of yellow soap and had to admit she was warming up to the man. *Everyone's got a smidgen of good in 'em*, Grandpa Wingate would say. Even a Danvers-Stiles?

Drying his hands with a dishcloth that had seen finer days, Julian led Holly into the combination living room-dining room. As she'd predicted, the views from the bank of windows were nothing short of stunning. The snow was deeper this far into the woods, clinging to the stone walls and evergreens.

Julian stirred the ashes in his stone fireplace with a wrought-iron poker and found a few red-hot coals. He added a stick of wood. She admired the way his body worked. His movements were casual. Natural. There was no wasted energy, nothing for show. He knew what he was doing and did it well.

He suited this practical, solid, attractive house. The strong native timbers and earthy colors told as much about him as Holly had learned from their conversations. He belonged here, she realized—and almost envied him. In all her wanderings, she'd never come to a place she couldn't envision leaving.

"Here, why don't you have a look at the goblets while I throw together some lunch." Before she could answer, he grabbed a black iron box and set it on the couch next to where she stood. "Enjoy."

When he returned to the kitchen, Holly sat on the edge of the couch. Her fingers were shaking. She didn't like that, but not because she was one to chastise herself for being nervous. As a storyteller, she'd had to learn to cope with—and accept—a degree of nervousness before a performance. No, she was being hard on herself because it wasn't nervousness that had set her hands to shaking. It wasn't even anticipation at seeing, at last, the fabled goblets of her childhood. It was guilt, pure and simple. She knew she was going to relieve Julian Stiles of them, and she was having her doubts about whether or not that was the right thing to do.

"Of course it is," she muttered. "His ancestors stole them from Zachariah!"

Her hands somewhat steadier, she opened the iron box.

"How do you like them?" Julian yelled from the kitchen.

She was breathless. "They're beautiful." Did she sound impressed but also suitably nonchalant? A professional's interest only? "They're so simple, and yet there's an understated elegance about them. And, of course, knowing Paul Revere crafted them adds to their aura."

He came into the kitchen doorway, the dish towel flung over one shoulder. "I'm going to put them on display in the restaurant—right out on the mantel in the main dining room—the old Danvers House parlor."

"You're kidding—a restaurant?" She knew she sounded appalled.

"It's not as gauche as it sounds. The Danvers House is too big to live in, and I don't want to turn it into apartments or a bed-and-breakfast. I have a couple of friends, a husband-wife team, who're chefs. They graduated from the culinary institute in Montpelier. They've been bouncing around, and now one's working up in Burlington and the other out in Saratoga Springs. They hardly see each other. They want to start a family, and they'd love to have their own restaurant. So we've worked out a deal."

The loss of the goblets, Holly thought, wouldn't have to affect those plans. They could still open their restaurant, start a family, be together. *You don't have to feel guilty!*

Julian disappeared back into the kitchen. "We're calling the place the Silver Goblets Restaurant. What do you think?"

"I think you should call it the Danvers House."

"How come?"

"That's what the house has been known as for the past couple of centuries, isn't it?"

"Yeah," he said thoughtfully, "I guess so. But we like the Silver Goblets. We figure we can put the story of the scandal—how Zachariah Wingate's misguided sense of pride drove him to steal the goblets to pay back his scholarship—right on the menu. When you have a couple of sterling-silver goblets crafted by Paul Revere himself, you ought to make use of them, right?"

"I suppose it'd be hard not to," Holly replied, her mouth dry as she stared at the beautiful goblets . . . and her spine stiffened. Just who did he think he was to jump to conclusions about her great-grandfather?

Julian materialized at her side, and she jumped, startled, as he unceremoniously handed her a sandwich, no napkin, no plate. "I've got paper towels if you want," he said.

"This'll be fine."

"It's Vermont smoked turkey."

All this politeness and chitchat was fraying her nerves—and she had the unmistakable feeling Julian wasn't entirely on the level with her. With her free hand, she snapped the iron case shut. "Aren't you afraid someone'll steal them?"

"From the restaurant?"

"Well, yes. I can't imagine anyone braving that driveway to steal them from here." *Oh, what a tangled web we weave . . .*

"I guess we'll have to figure out something for security, but I'm not worried about it, no."

She looked him square in his emerald eyes. He was one sexy male. "You must have changed your opinion of me since we first met."

He shrugged, biting into his sandwich. "What, should I be afraid you're going to try to steal the goblets?"

His eyes held hers, his brows slightly raised, and she could feel her throat tightening. She wished he would stop looking at her like that, so knowingly, daring her. My God, she thought, *does* he know?

"Of course not. You were just so suspicious when I crashed through your ceiling—"

"What a bastard I am," he said with amused sarcasm. "A strange woman breaks into my building, misses me by mere inches falling through my ceiling, takes off when I catch her in a lie about a couple of lost puppies and I get suspicious."

"Now you know I'm just a storyteller and . . ."

"And it was just your storyteller's curiosity that drove you to breaking into the Danvers House. It won't wash, Holly." Without preamble, he headed back to the kitchen, returning with a paper towel. "Honey mustard on your cheek. Want me to get it?"

She snatched her paper towel. "I will, thanks."

A flash of laughter in his eyes told her he'd noticed how quickly and forcefully she'd gone for the towel, knew it meant she wasn't anxious to have him touch her. Or, more accurately, was too anxious.

He went on, as if there'd been no honey mustard and no paper towel, "I just don't think you're a thief."

"I'm not," she said, forcing herself not to look away. "Good."

And you're not as nice as you're pretending you are. Holly inhaled, maintaining her self-control. She'd been lured into the forest on the wolf's terms. Her! Grandpa Wingate had warned her about the devils in Millbrook, Vermont! Of all people, she should have known better than to let herself get sucked in by a little Yankee charm just because Julian Stiles had decided to act nice.

"Coffee?" he asked—so charmingly.

"Sure."

Again he disappeared into the kitchen, grabbing the telephone when it rang. "Hey, Adam—what's up?" he asked. "No kidding. Yeah, I'm on my way." He hung up, calling into the living room, "That was my brother. Something's come up at the mill and I've got to head back."

Holly was on her feet, making her way to the kitchen. "Nothing serious, I hope?"

"To Adam everything that concerns the mill's serious—but no, nothing serious. Just pressing. I'm sorry to have to cut our lunch short. Look, why don't you just make yourself at home? The kitchen's not very complicated. There's coffee, tea, cocoa, beer. Help yourself. If you'd like another sandwich—"

Her stomach was in such a knot, she could barely choke down the one she had. It was her turn to be royally suspicious. "No, no, I'm fine."

"You'll be able to find your way out all right?"

She nodded. "I can leave now if you'd rather . . ."

"No, I wouldn't rather."

There was something serious, something seductive, in his expression that Holly warned herself not to examine more closely. "My van's blocking your Rover—"

"I'll just take the truck."

He was dripping sweetness. Holly decided to go along and play his game. "And I should just hang out here as long as I want?"

"Yes," he said. "Spend the afternoon, if you like. When I get back we can go out together and have an early dinner."

"Then I'd have to come all the way back here and drive out on that two-point-three mile driveway in the pitch-dark alone. I'm afraid I'd have a wreck."

He shrugged, his eyes fixed on hers, the something serious, something seductive easily detected now: the man wanted her. "You could wait and go in the morning."

Before she could stop herself, she glanced around. The small house couldn't have more than one bedroom. Julian watched her, and she could tell he knew what she was thinking. A night alone with him here in the woods . . . him on the couch, her in his bed . . . vice versa. She felt herself stiffening against the onslaught of images. It would never work. With the sexual electricity snapping and popping between them, they'd end up making love. And regretting it afterward. They were just too different. She was a wandering Texas storyteller. He was a stick-in-the-mud Yankee.

And a Danvers-Stiles to boot.

"Are you serious," she said, "or just teasing?"

"What do you think?" He smiled and moved closer to her, his eyes strangely dark, and hooded. "Let's stop pretending there's nothing going on between us."

"Julian—"

"I can feel it, Holly. So can you."

She could. She wouldn't deny it, at least not to herself. To him, she said, "Most of my things are at your aunt's house—"

"Holly, Holly."

He brushed a strawberry lock behind her ear, let his fingers comb gently through her hair to her nape. His touch was light, tantalizing. His fingertips gently pressed the soft, sensitive skin just under her hairline. Her tensed shoulder and neck muscles loosened, and she responded unexpectedly with a soft, contented moan and closed her eyes, for a moment giving in to the pleasure of what he was doing.

"I wish I understood you," he whispered.

She could feel his breath on her mouth. He brushed his lips on hers. If she opened her eyes, she knew she'd have to make him stop, so she kept them closed. His lips touched her nose, her eyelids. His kisses were soft, feathery, as impossible to catch as the wind. Before she could react to his kissing one spot, he was on to another, until finally he came back to her mouth, and he lingered there.

"I'll stop if you want me to," he said.

She shook her head, opening her eyes now, refusing to try to hide from her own responsibility for what was happening. "I don't."

Slowly, erotically, he moved his hand from her hairline down her spine to her waist. He drew her closer, or she pulled herself against him—it didn't matter which. She wasn't keeping a scorecard.

Then his mouth opened on hers, and he traced her lips with the hot wetness of his tongue. Her entire body seemed to gasp with the sheer awareness of him, the excitement he was creating in her.

There was no denying her hunger now. No pretending, no holding back. She opened her mouth, inviting the darting heat of his tongue, and with her tongue, she traced his lips, the sharp edges of his teeth. She could feel her breasts swelling, straining within the confines of her bra, begging for the touch of his hands, the wet fire of his tongue.

Then he pulled away, as quickly and abruptly as if she'd just turned into a live coal and was suddenly too hot to handle.

His gaze was dusky, filled with bridled passion. Holly was no fool: she knew he wanted her.

Knew, too, that she wanted him.

"Stay here as long as you like," he said, a little hoarse.

Holly decided not to ask him what the hell had just happened, what it meant. What had happened, they'd kissed. What it meant, nothing.

Quit kidding yourself!

But she said, "Should I lock up when I leave?"

"You don't have to." He cleared his throat. "Pen and Ink would take care of any strangers, so it's only you I'd have to worry about. And since I'm leaving you here alone, I guess I'm not worried about you swiping the crystal—not that I have any."

"I can't imagine you'd need any," she replied tonelessly.

"No silver, either—except for the goblets."

"They'd be easy to trace, though."

"They would indeed."

Indeed, Holly thought. Indeed, indeed.

There was something.

Something in his eyes, in his half smile. In his tone, too controlled, too deliberate. In the way he looked at her that extra second or two. In his stance, confident, challenging.

The bastard knows you're going to take back the goblets, she thought. *He knows!*

How?

He's leaving you here alone so he can double back and catch you red-handed stealing the goblets.

Just as sure as she herself knew her name was Holly Wingate Paynter, she was sure Julian Stiles knew it, too. She was trained to observe, analyze and imitate the smallest expression, the tiniest movement. As good as Julian was, she had him figured out now.

He had his hook baited and all she had to do was bite.

His departure—leaving her there alone—was the fat, juicy worm on the end of his sharp hook. She wasn't supposed to be able to resist.

She rose in a regal sweep. "On second thought," she said, with a disarming smile, "I think I'll just head back to town now. There's not much to do up here alone, and I'd feel a little awkward staying without you. Thanks for lunch."

His expression didn't change. No disappointment, no pride—nothing. Oh, he was good. He said as if he meant it, "Anytime."

On her way out, Holly resisted one last glance at the iron box holding the silver goblets. She didn't care what Julian Stiles knew or didn't know. She didn't even care about righting a hundred-year-old wrong against the Wingate family. Now her own pride was at stake. Had the kiss been part of the lure? She hated to think so, but who was she to figure how far a Danvers-Stiles would go? If Grandpa Wingate had still been around, he'd have told her.

She didn't like being baited.

She'd be back.

JULIAN ALMOST LANDED in the swamp himself. Preoccupied with one strawberry-haired, blue-eyed, glib-tongued, determined Texan, he got going too fast. His left front tire hit the ice, and he spun out, whipping around a full one-hundred-eighty degrees. Only luck and the snowbank kept him on the road. He could imagine what Holly Paynter would have done if she'd come upon him sinking into the icy swamp. He'd never hear the end of it.

After a series of maneuvers, he inched his way back around and continued, paying better attention. Holly had decided to follow him in her van, but he'd lost her. Either he was going too fast for her or she had doubled back to swipe the goblets.

He wouldn't bet on either scenario.

When he came to the end of his notorious driveway, he pulled out of sight.

In a few minutes, Holly's dark green van puttered cautiously past him. She was hanging on to the steering wheel with both hands and watching the road. Once she reached the main road, she speeded up. He could almost hear her sigh of relief.

Julian kept his eyes on her bumper until it disappeared around a bend. She couldn't have been that far behind him. Had she had time to sneak back to the house?

"You're carrying this thing too damned far," he muttered.

But he could still feel her warmth and softness, could still taste her. She'd wanted him as much as he'd wanted her. There was no question of that. The nonsense about the goblets was just a game, he thought. An excuse to act like a couple of adolescents while they sorted out what else was crackling between them.

He backed out into the road, swerved around and headed back up his driveway, taking it as fast as he dared. What the hell, he thought, he had to be sure.

Leaving his truck running, he dashed inside.

The goblets were still there, gleaming inside the iron box.

He frowned. What was Holly Paynter up to?

If he'd been interested in prevention, he'd have tucked the goblets under his arm and kept them there. But he wasn't. He was interested in . . .

"Her," he said under his breath.

Holly Paynter was what he was interested in. He wanted to know if she'd go as far as stealing the goblets, what she'd do with them, why she wanted them.

He wanted to know her.

More simply, he wanted her.

"Hell."

He shut the iron box and dropped it back on the couch, where she'd left it. Then he climbed back into his truck and took the ride out to the main road nice and slow. Holly was on to him. What he needed now, he thought, was another plan.

Or to confront her honestly with this obsession he had with her. What he felt about her. Somehow, though, he didn't think she was ready for that. And perhaps neither was he. Honesty would entail soul-searching, long talks, deepening ties and commitment. Holly Paynter by her own admission was a wanderer, and he knew himself well enough by now to know he wasn't. He liked his life in Millbrook. It was here he belonged. Start bringing this stuff up now instead of goblets, and he didn't know what would happen.

Simply put, he didn't want to risk losing her. Not yet. So he'd go on figuring out exactly what she was doing in town. Figuring about the goblets, her status as a Wingate, teasing, luring…and perhaps, finally, having her.

"No." Adam Stiles had to yell to be heard above the saws in the new building. He'd never been one to mince words. Without even glancing at his younger brother, he headed back outside. Julian followed. He was accustomed to Adam's recalcitrance.

"I'm not asking you to commit perjury," Julian said as they headed down the short, sanded path back to the main building. "It's not as if you'd be lying to Congress or the Internal Revenue Service."

"I'd still be lying."

"To a thief."

"What's she stolen?"

"Nothing yet, but—"

"Then how do you know she's a thief."

"Trust me."

"If I were you, I'd just put the goblets in a bank vault and forget about them." Adam stopped at the lower-level door to the old sawmill and, his eyes even paler in the bright sun, looked at Julian. "But that wouldn't be as much fun would it?"

Julian grinned; his brother did know him. "I guess not."

"Entrapment's illegal."

"For a law enforcement officer."

"Then it's unfair."

"True."

"But you've given her enough chances?"

"Too many."

Adam sighed. "I don't like playing games. I called you with that fake emergency like we agreed. Even that was going too far if you ask me. What're you going to do if she does steal the goblets?"

"Catch her."

"And then what? No." He winced. "Forget I asked. I'm not sure I want to know."

With that, Adam went inside, chuckling as he headed over to the water-powered saw with the extra-long carriage, his favorite. Julian wondered what the hell his brother thought was so funny. The man could be damned irritating. Here he was trying to nab a thief and—

And, of course, he was having the time of his life.

"You'll cover for me?" he called to his brother.

Adam waved his hand in assent, as if to say, *Don't I always?* And it was true; he did. Julian gave a mock-salute and trotted upstairs, trying to keep the spring out of his step and telling himself that all he was doing was protecting his property and going after a blue-eyed, lying Texan.

Yeah, bud, but to what end?

He left the question hanging, and got to work.

5

HOLLY STRIPPED DOWN to her underwear and collapsed onto the big brass bed of her room at the Windham House, sinking into the soft, billowing down comforter. It was almost teatime, but she'd never make it. Her stomach hurt and her heart was pounding.

It had been just too easy.

She stared at the ceiling in an effort to regain her increasingly elusive calm. If she shut her eyes, she'd imagine things she didn't want to imagine. Julian Stiles, for one. He'd begun to dominate her thinking.

Several additional guests had arrived at the Windham House, coming up from New York City and Boston for weekend skiing. Holly had fancied herself mingling with them over tea, laughing, observing her first group of urban skiers.

Instead she was upstairs...alone...feeling unsettled and faintly apprehensive.

But she did have the goblets.

"Whoopee," she said, dispirited.

She'd gotten them back just like she'd promised herself she would. Grandpa Wingate would have been proud, and Great-grandfather Zachariah could rest in peace. It wasn't as if they were Stiles or Danvers family heirlooms. Julian, like everyone else in Millbrook, had assumed up until he accidentally found them buried in the Danvers House cellar that the goblets were long gone—stolen by Zachariah. This just wasn't a case of finders keepers. Morally the goblets didn't belong to any member of the Danvers or Stiles clans. They belonged with the Wingates.

A moot point now. Possession was nine-tenths of the law, it was said, and Holly had them.

She should be celebrating!

But it had been too easy. *Nothing* was ever easy for her. Luck, fortune, winning sweepstakes—all that was for other people. What she got in life, she had to earn.

Even with her eyes wide open, she could vividly picture Julian standing on a stepladder in this room on a hot summer afternoon, his chest bare, stark-white ceiling paint splattered over his tanned arms and shoulders. It was an unwanted, troubling image. Millbrook Academy alumnus though he was, he wasn't afraid of a good day's work. And he was the kind of man who helped a widowed aunt turn her house into a bed-and-breakfast; who was transforming an old house into a restaurant not just for investment purposes, but to help two friends.

Holly couldn't help wondering what might have happened if she'd just laid out the Wingate version of that night a hundred years ago. Had explained to Julian she'd come to Millbrook to right that old, old wrong against her great-grandfather? Maybe he'd have agreed that Paul Revere had intended the goblets for the Wingates, that they belonged with her, as Zachariah's only direct descendant, to pass along to her children and grandchildren.

Holly snorted at her own weakness. She hadn't *stolen* the goblets. Not exactly. She was merely in the process of restoring them to their rightful owner—herself. And only because she was Zachariah's only direct descendant. She wasn't acting out of avarice, just a compulsion to do what was right.

She heard the faint sound of a car door banging shut outside. Another weekend skier arriving? Holly relished the interruption of her uncontrolled thoughts and attack of guilt—and no small measure of anxiety.

Had she stolen the goblets just to have Julian after her again? Because he was getting too close—or not close enough? She wanted to scream with frustration! Her feelings were all a jumble and . . .

"And, hell's bells, you just *know* it was too damned easy."

She tried to think about the skiers downstairs. Holly had never been on skis in her life and couldn't quite figure out why anyone would want to go screaming down the side of a mountain on two skinny waxed boards. *You prefer to get your kicks out of stealing from perfect strangers!*

"You didn't steal from anyone!" she chastised herself aloud.

And certainly not from a stranger. She'd been hearing about Millbrook and the Danvers and Stiles clans all her life. Somehow Julian didn't feel like a stranger, nor even the arch enemy she'd anticipated. In a way, she felt as if she'd known him a good part of her life.

She remembered the feel of his mouth on hers, the warmth and hardness of him, and shuddered with a longing so keen, so fierce, she wanted to cry out.

Another door slammed. Even in the attic, Holly could hear fast, hard footsteps.

She bolted upright. "It's him!"

A small voice told her she was being paranoid, but that was naïveté talking. She damned well knew who was coming up after her. And here she'd been feeling guilty! Julian Stiles could damn well take care of himself.

She could hear him taking the stairs in leaps and bounds.

"Oh, Lordy..."

Reenergized, she threw her feet down off the bed and looked around wildly for evidence of what she'd been up to the previous hour. There was nothing; she'd been extremely careful. She could plot and scheme with the best. Satisfied, she jumped up and grabbed her fine cotton kimono-style robe, wishing she had something more substantial she could throw on fast. Sure her door was closed, but would that stop Julian Stiles? In his place, would it stop her?

She had just enough time to tie her robe before he barged in without so much as a knock or by-your-leave. He did, however, shut the door behind him. His eyes were blazing, his jaw set, his fists clenched. It wasn't difficult to guess he'd been by his house and found his precious goblets gone—and had decided whom to blame.

Of course, he'd have no proof. Holly had seen to that.

She decided to feign innocence. "Julian, what on earth..."

He took her in with a sweeping look that might not have phased her had it been merely predatory, angry, know-it-all—and it was all of those things. But, disconcertingly, there was satisfaction there as well and something else she couldn't quite pinpoint—respect, maybe? As if she'd done exactly what he'd expected her to do. And being a hard case himself, he would notice, and possibly admire, a degree of relentlessness in others. She had come to Millbrook for the goblets and now she had them. There was a certain uncompromising logic to that that he'd understand. She just didn't know how far it would get her.

"Don't start." His teeth were clenched so tightly together he had trouble getting the words out; his jumble of emotions was raging and he was fighting like mad to hang on. "You fell for the bait, Holly. Hook, line and sinker."

Stifling a wave of alarm, Holly faked a yawn and stretched her arms up over her as if just awakening from a long, peaceful nap. A deliberate calm was her best defense—possibly her only defense.

"If you want to talk," she said, "by all means, let's talk. But I'll tell you right now, I haven't the faintest idea of what you're getting at."

He laughed, unswayed by her manufactured innocence. "You can stop right there because you're not going to talk your way out of this one."

It was difficult for Holly not to regard his words as a direct challenge. She could talk her way out of *anything*. Grandpa Wingate had told her so often enough. She gestured to the rocker. "Why don't you sit down and tell me what happened?"

"You're good," he admitted grudgingly. "You can make yourself look relaxed even when you've got to be shaking in your socks. I've got you this time and you damned well know it."

"Shaking in my socks? *Me?*" She scoffed, adding, "If there's one thing that doesn't scare me, it's you."

"I'm not talking about fear, I'm talking about nervousness—anticipation."

"About what?"

Again that near-humorless laugh. "Oh, so innocent."

"Mr. Stiles—"

"Make it Julian. You can't start pulling back now."

"Pulling back from what?"

His eyes were too dark, fathomless pits. "From me."

She drew back abruptly, her concentration shattered, and stumbled on her own shoes. She had to put a hand down on the bed to steady herself because she knew he was right. Ever since she had crashed down on top of him at the Danvers House, they'd been egging each other on. They could claim the purest of motives: he was protecting his property, even Millbrook, from an unscrupulous storyteller; she was trying to right a wrong committed against her family. But they could have accomplished their tasks in other, less directly confrontational ways—without the sexual electricity, the zest for contact on any level, at nearly any price.

She'd been waiting for him, she realized. Restoring the goblets to the Wingate hands had a lot less to do with family pride now than it had a week ago. The goblets had become a way of intensifying what was going on between her and Julian—of bringing him closer to her, forcing him to show her what he was made of.

To show her that what was going on between them was real.

"Don't be ridiculous," she said, sounding stuffy and self-conscious.

His gaze drifted over her. Oh, for a flannel robe! The lines of her body were etched plainly against the thin cotton of her kimono, which showed too much neck, too much bare leg. Her skin tingled. Her eyes locked with his, just for an instant, long enough for her to see the burning in his.

Glancing around, she suddenly saw the lacy bra hanging on the bathroom doorknob...the full slip and sheer stockings neatly folded at the foot of the bed for tonight... the lipstick left open on the dresser. They were small, personal things. The kinds of things that had, in a few short days, made this cozy, pretty attic suite, guest room or not, her space. Julian had invaded it. It was as if he were inside her, looking around, checking her out, uncovering all her secrets.

The image had such sensual overtones she could feel her cheeks flushing and her mouth going dry. Her attraction to him was fly in the ointment enough. She didn't need him to notice—or respond in kind. *A little late for that, babes*, she thought. And who did she think she was kidding? Certainly not herself. Her attraction to him, she was beginning to think, wasn't the fly in the ointment; it was everything.

"We've only known each other a few days," she said.

He moved another step toward her, so tantalizingly close. "Time's got nothing to do with it. I think you know that. What's going on between us—"

"No—no, Julian, this has to stop. There's nothing going on between us, all right? I don't know what you're trying to do here. I haven't known you long enough even to guess. Perhaps you've been living out in the woods alone for too long and seeing a new face makes you . . ." She paused, shrugging her shoulders, wondering if she'd gone off the deep end. "I don't know, weird or something."

He'd unclenched his fists, and she could see his callused palms and his strong fingers. Her monologue to the contrary, she imagined them on the soft swell of her breasts. *Oh, Lordy.*

He was standing toe-to-toe with her, his breathing hard. His eyes, so dark all of a sudden, were squinted as if in bright sun, searching her face for all the kinds of things she didn't want him to see. She prided herself on her ability to read people, but she couldn't read him, not now. Was he more angry than satisfied? More amused than incredulous? More determined than put off? She couldn't tell.

"All right," he said calmly. "We won't talk about what's between us. We'll save that for later and talk about the goblets now."

Holly took some comfort in knowing her instincts hadn't failed her: she'd guessed her heist had been too blasted easy! But how much did Julian know? What should she admit? Early on in life, she'd learned not to change a story midstream, not to grab for another piece of floating debris that seemed stronger than the one you had, but might not be. Why take the risk of sinking? What she'd told Julian so far might be garbage, but it was her garbage and so far it had kept her afloat.

Licking her lips, she managed an innocent, "The goblets?" She coughed, clearing her throat, and could almost hear Grandpa Wingate urging her not to let the likes of a Danvers-Stiles get to her. *You cannot fall for this man!* "What about them? Are they the reason you barged in here?"

He gave her a smile that reminded her of her grandfather's stories about the devils who'd run his daddy out of town. "Cut the innocent-me act, Holly. The *last* thing you are is innocent. You came to Millbrook to steal my Paul Revere goblets, didn't you?"

His goblets! The sheer conceit of his assumptions— never mind their general accuracy—galvanized her into taking the offensive. "I'm no thief, Julian. I'll be damned if I'm going to stand here and listen to you fling insults and accusations. Obviously you've jumped to some kind of outrageous conclusion about me, but that's really your concern, not mine." She was steamed now . . . and concerned. *What's the bastard up to?* Oh, but he did have a way of keeping her interest, didn't he? In a deliberately snooty voice she said, "I'll thank you to get out of my room."

She started past him toward the door, but he caught her around the middle. Before she could say a word or even move, his touch sent hundreds of fiery sensations burning through her. She could feel the hard length of his arm against her back; could feel herself melting into him. *Nothing's easy for a Wingate, remember?*

"I won't stand for insults," she told him, her mouth dry.

"What about the truth?"

"I don't need you to tell me the truth."

"Holly . . ." His voice was husky, his mouth so very close to hers that she could feel the heat of his breath, of her own wanting. "You're making me crazy."

"No crazier than you're making me."

His grip on her remained firm but not, to her distress, unpleasant. If she'd sensed even a borderline physical threat from him, she would have sent him marching. She would have the irrevocable excuse she needed to believe he wasn't the man for her. Nonthreatening though it was, his hold on her wasn't exactly open and loving, either. It was . . . knowing, she thought. And tightly controlled. As if he were on fire just a little himself.

She considered kissing him, but held back. *Common sense, m'dear*, she thought. First, the goblets.

"Oh, hell," he muttered, and dropped his arm. "Let's get this goblet business over with first."

"I agree. Absolutely. Let's. What goblet business?"

He sighed. "Holly, I know who you are."

"I should hope so. I've been completely forthcoming—"

"Like hell. You're a thieving Wingate."

He was staring right at her so she had to be extra careful; if he'd still had a hand on her, she'd never have been able to pull off her look of total mystification. "A who?"

"Your name is Holly *Wingate* Paynter."

"I know that. It's no big secret. Wingate's just a name—"

"Your parents picked it out of a hat?"

"A telephone book," she said, ignoring his sarcasm. He was being so smug, he deserved whatever lies she told him. Thought he had her, did he? Not by a long shot! "If you want to talk to me, you'll have to go downstairs. I'll join you in a minute. We can have tea and discuss this without—without all the fireworks."

He laughed, truly amused. "Darling, if you think what's gone on between us so far is fireworks, you'd better get yourself ready for one hell of an explosion. We've only just begun. And I'm not letting you out of my sight. I think you probably believe you have a damn good reason for doing what you've done, but I can't be sure you won't be out the window and on your way back to Texas before I ever see you downstairs. We'll talk right here."

"About my name?" She shrugged, trying to look bored; her heart, however, was skipping beats. "I think it's English, I'm not sure. But I gather you're intrigued by the coincidence of it being Wingate?"

"I am."

"Well, that's all it is: a coincidence. I suppose having Wingate as a middle name might have helped the article on your rediscovery of the goblets catch my eye, but that's all I'll admit."

"Don't lie to me, Holly. You're only making this tougher on both of us."

Yeah, she'd bet it was real tough on him. "I'm not..."

"You stole the goblets."

She bit the insides of her cheeks to keep herself from saying something rash and stared at him. He stared back. Again his expression was impossible to read. There was smugness in the curve of his mouth, anger in the flush of his cheeks. Yet his eyes had softened, their dark green warming, and in them she thought she could sense a stubborn attraction to her . . . and, once more, that curious satisfaction and admiration. Maybe it was just her imagination. Wishful thinking. Her survival instincts overstepping the bounds of reality.

"I stole the goblets," she repeated, her tone disbelieving but mild, as if his accusation was too far-fetched for her to get upset about. "That's a pretty wild thought. They're not at your house, I take it?"

"They are not." He was back to that tight-lipped way of talking.

Holly shook her head, exhaling in apparent commiseration. "Wow, that's too bad. You know, it isn't very nice of you to assume I'm responsible. Just because coincidentally my middle name happens to be Wingate, and I went out to your house—at your invitation, I might add—to have a look at the goblets earlier today doesn't make me the thief."

"Give it up."

She sank onto the edge of the bed and put all she had into looking terribly, terribly hurt and confused. "I don't understand—why would you think I would steal anything? Julian, I'm a successful storyteller. I have a reputation to maintain. Why on earth would I risk that on stealing from you? Just because you didn't believe my lost puppies story the other day doesn't mean I'm responsible for every nasty going-on in Millbrook." She lifted her shoulders in despair and let them fall as she exhaled. "You really have misjudged me, you know."

"Sweetheart, this time I knew enough to get all my ducks in a row before I tried to take you on."

He bent over and placed his hands on his thighs, steadying himself as he looked right into her eyes. His mouth was maybe three inches from hers. She wondered—nuttily—what he'd do if she kissed him.

"I saw you," he said.

Her hands and feet went numb, and she could feel the blood draining out of her face. Had he—or was he just bluffing, trying to lure her into confessing? She called upon lessons learned from a childhood of perpetually being caught red-handed and an adulthood of telling stories for a living. Getting her feet into boiling water was a bad habit of hers; getting them out again was a passion—and a particular skill.

It was time Julian Danvers Stiles discovered what she was made of. Time to do something before he hauled her off to jail!

She sat up straight and tightened the tie on her kimono robe. Too much bare skin was showing. She had goose bumps on her forearms and calves—and not because of the cold. January in Vermont was not the same as January in central Florida, but sitting there under Julian Stiles's scrutiny, Holly felt plenty warm. *It's all that boiling water I'm in, not just him.* But here she was, neck deep in the proverbial bubbling cauldron, thinking about what it would be like to trace a finger along that Yankee chin of his.

"Tell me, Julian," she said, very cool under the circumstances, "exactly what did you see?"

He straightened up, and she forced herself to give him a good, objective once-over. Physically the man was rock solid. Hard through the middle, big through the shoulders, lean and strong in the legs. She'd already felt his arms and they'd passed muster. Or not muster, really. Strength and fitness were desirable in anyone, man or woman, but it was a person's mind that intrigued her most. And how was Julian Danvers Stiles mentally? She sighed: rock solid. Didn't need a soul. Lived in the woods all alone. Could take care of himself. Dealt with the world on his own terms. Didn't cotton to liars and cheats, but didn't expect them at every turn, either. Deal with me straight up, he would probably say, and I'll do the same with you. Cross me and—

You're in trouble, HP, she thought.

Just like always.

"I saw you drive up to my house," he told her, his voice a low, uncompromising growl. "I saw you park your beat-up van in my driveway. And I saw you trot your fanny into my living room, grab my goblets and leave with one hell of a triumphant look on your face." He pointed a finger at her, just for emphasis. "*That's* what I saw."

"Well, bully for you, but maybe I *have* made you crazy. Going down that driveway of yours once was enough for me. And if it's just your word against mine, who's to say who'd believe whom?"

She might not have even uttered a word. "Where did you stash them?" he asked.

"Really," she said, leaning back on her elbows. A dumb move. Her robe fell open and exposed more cleavage than she had intended. Another inch and he'd have a view of two freezing cold pink nipples. From the sudden sultriness of Julian's gaze, she guessed he was thinking much the same, a complication for them both. Much better to counter charges of theft clothed head to toe in something bleak and opaque. Pretending not to notice, Holly continued, "Search my room, if you want. Search my van. Search *me*—" A mistake. She caught it too late.

"Don't tempt me." His voice was husky, his eyes smoldering. Still, he was in a business-first mood. "But I don't need to. I know what I saw."

Just like 1889, Holly thought. A Wingate's word against that of a Danvers and a Stiles. Had Zachariah been telling a tale then, the way she was now? Impossible. Grandpa Wingate had insisted the goblets had been given to his ancestor by Paul Revere himself.

"I'm a very thorough man, Holly," Julian told her. "It's something I wouldn't forget, if I were you."

Damn right she wouldn't.

"It's your word against mine," he pointed out.

And she thought she'd been so clever returning to the Windham House, playing the innocent. Who'd think a thief would stick around town?

Julian didn't need to think anything. His damn sneaky ways had done all the thinking for him.

She sighed heavily. "May I ask you one question?"

"Sure." He was being magnanimous.

"You caught me red-handed, right?"

He smiled nastily. "I'd say so."

"Then why didn't you come out of hiding and ask me what the devil I was doing instead of lurking about like some kind of sleazy Peeping Tom?" She lifted her feet onto the bed and tucked herself into the tailor position, carefully arranging her kimono so it didn't reveal anything more than he could already see. "That's pretty low."

"I wanted to give you time to hang yourself."

"I see. And to change my mind?"

"That, too."

"And, of course, to see what I'd do next."

"Right."

"In other words, you wanted me to dig my own hole and jump in it headfirst. You set me up. You got Adam to cover for you. Your own brother. He told me you weren't going to be around the rest of the afternoon, that you'd gone out to a site with a client and wouldn't be back until early evening. Gave me plenty of leeway, didn't you? I should have taken my sweet time, made you freeze your buns off out there waiting for me—"

"You could have taken the whole damned night," he said. "I was dressed for a wait."

"Where were you?"

"Behind the woodshed. I thought the dogs were going to give me away, but they didn't."

She'd wondered why Pen and Ink had virtually ignored her. Good with animals, she'd come prepared with dog biscuits, but they'd only barked mildly at her arrival before going back and sniffing around the woodshed. If she'd been a more experienced thief, she wouldn't have marveled at her good fortune and instead have realized something nasty was afoot...namely one Julian Danvers Stiles.

She frowned, studying him. She didn't like the look on his face. He was holding back something. But what could he possibly have left out? Then she saw he was trying to keep from grinning. The bastard was enjoying himself!

Buster, she thought, *you're in for it now.*

"You didn't take me up to your place today just to have lunch," she told him. "Uh-uh. You were luring me into your trap. You knew this Wingate stuff had piqued my storyteller's interest, and you saw your chance to get even with me for crashing through your ceiling and telling you about those lost puppies, then running off on you." This time she pointed a finger at him. "That's called entrapment."

"You can call what I did anything you want," he said. "What *you* did everybody in Millbrook will call stealing."

"Oh, I doubt that."

"Why doesn't that surprise me? But spare me another of your tales. I want the goblets back, Holly, and unless you want to be straight with me and tell me everything, then you can pack up and get out of town."

She refused to take him seriously. "Playing hardball this time, I see."

"Maybe it's just time you were honest with me."

Honesty, she thought, would mean an end to the game—to whatever was going on between them. She'd have to explain about Grandpa Wingate and his railings against Julian's family, the hundred-year-old wrong his ancestors had committed against hers. She'd have to leave Millbrook, with or without the goblets. And she wasn't ready to give up just yet. *But what if he's just asking you to be yourself so you can work things out?*

It was a risk she wasn't yet prepared to take. She couldn't bear the idea of all this ending now, like this.

"Well, I can't say I blame you," she said airily. "What I did this afternoon must look terribly. . . suspicious to you. But I acted out of purely honorable motives. Would you like me to explain?"

"Do I have a choice?"

He seemed almost amused, and she took heart. "You're going to end up looking like an ass if I don't."

"Happens to the best of us. Spare me, Holly. What about the goblets?"

"As you wish. Do you want to go with me to get them?"

"You think I'd let you go alone?"

"No, not really."

"We have to go outside, I take it."

"Mmm." She admired how unconcerned she sounded. What if she'd met her match? Zachariah Wingate hadn't been able to handle it when a Danvers and a Stiles had ganged up on him. Julian was both, two Wingate enemies rolled into one.

"Here, then." He looked around and got her pants, handing them to her. "Where's your shirt?"

"I'll get it. You don't have to dress me."

It was the wrong thing to say. Or maybe the right thing, if she wanted to know where he stood on the subject of the sexual tension crackling between them like a downed electrical wire—dangerous and very alive. They'd both been jumping around, dodging, doing everything to keep from stepping on it. Now they had, unintentionally. And finally, at last, she had it confirmed—and so did he—that the stolen goblets had

damned little to do with why he was here. With what
he had against her, he'd have gone to the police if there
wasn't something else at work. He looked at her for a
long time. She considered a hundred different com-
ments she could make. Sexy, flirtatious, stuffy, coy, innocent. Confrontational. None seemed right—honest.
She didn't know why, but here she was in the middle of
one of the biggest tales she'd ever told, and she was
concerned with honesty, if not about facts and partic-
ulars, at least about feelings.

In the end, she said nothing,. and he said fine, she
could get dressed. He'd wait outside in the hall, which
he did. The moment had passed. *We're not going to
talk*, Holly thought, more frustrated than she'd have
imagined possible. *We never will. We're just going to
keep on like this, him a Danvers-Stiles, me a Wingate,
pushing and fighting and—what difference does it
make? I must be crazy to think there ever could be anything between the two of us.*

There couldn't be, she reminded herself. What they
were doing now was just a game. An amusing way to
pass the time during her brief stay in southern Vermont.

Her throat tightened at the prospect of having to
leave. What was happening to her?

She put on her pants and a shirt, threw a wooly
sweater over it, and added two pairs of socks. Her feet
felt as if they'd never get warm again. And here she was,
venturing back out into the January cold. It was lu-
nacy. Why'd she have to see that damned article in the
Orlando newspaper?

Maybe it was fate....

She couldn't get into her gum shoes fast enough. when she was ready, she opened the door and smiled at Julian, who hadn't, of course, given up on her and gone home. "We can take my van," she told him.

"This better not be a trick."

She only smiled, not feeling the least bit guilty. He was getting an inside look at how Holly Wingate Paynter worked, and there were those in the world who'd consider that not a trick, but a marvelous treat.

It was his own loss, she told herself, that he probably wasn't among them. Then again, with him, who knew?

6

JULIAN WAS GLAD to let Holly drive. Jousting with her in the guest room at the Windham House had taken its toll. He was distracted—probably crazy, he thought. And he was getting his first look inside her van, inside a part of her life he hadn't yet seen. She had everything in there: clothes, books, files, posters, tape recorder, insulated cooler, boxes of Cheerios and sugarless cookies, blankets, Thermos. She'd even hung curtains on the back side windows.

His eyes kept drifting to the cot in back, and he thought...knew...that one day he'd make love to her there. He'd bet it'd be sooner rather than later.

Despite having this self-described Sun Belt type behind the wheel, Julian wasn't worried as they sped along the winding, unlit road into the dark, cold hills up beyond Old Millbrook, in the general direction of the sawmill. She could still detour to his house—or anywhere.

He told himself as long as the goblets were at the end of the journey, he didn't care where she took him.

And yet he knew better.

If the goblets were his only concern—or even his prime concern—he'd never have done what he'd done. He wouldn't even be here now, sitting next to her in her wild van. He'd have called the damned police.

He *had* set her up. She'd been right about that.

Yet if all he'd meant to do was protect what was his, he would never have risked that she'd skip town before he could get back to the Windham House. He'd have confronted her back at his house before she'd run off with the goblets in the first place.

The truth was, he didn't really give a damn about the goblets. They'd been a fortuitous discovery, that was all.

What he gave a damn about was this beautiful storyteller with her devastatingly blue eyes. Why had she lied to him? Why did the goblets mean so much to her?

More particularly, why was she refusing to acknowledge what was going on between them?

He also wanted to know what was going on with himself. The source of this mad obsession with her. What it would drive him to do to his life—to hers. Whether he had any business—any *right*—to continue to play games with this woman.

And the goblets were a game. A device. A way into Holly Paynter's mind, and maybe her heart. He just didn't know if that was a responsible game to be playing. He gave her a sideways glance. She was a good driver; she obviously spent a great deal of time on the road. *A wanderer.*

He said dryly, "You're awfully quiet."

She grinned. "You sound suspicious."

"I'm just assuming you're plotting and scheming how you're going to get yourself out of this one."

"Not at all. I don't have anything to say right now, although I do admit I rarely go very long without saying something."

"That I can believe."

"Even when I'm by myself, lots of times I'll pop a cassette in my recorder and just start describing what I see and feel as I'm driving. Sound crazy?"

"Now that I'm getting to know you, no."

She negotiated a sharp upward curve, her eyes on the road, her hair sticking out in as many different directions as possible. She didn't look pale or nervous or particularly guilty. Not even irritated. Just very determined. *She's got something up her sleeve.* Julian sat back, smiling. In his opinion, determination was a major measure of character. Were lost puppies going to come into it again? Whatever she was cooking up, she was bound to try to make him feel like a worm because *she* stole a pair of sterling-silver goblets from *him*.

He couldn't wait for her next move.

"This van is something else," he said, looking around. "You could live in here."

"Sometimes it feels as if I do, but actually, I have an apartment in Houston. As I think I told you, between performances and research I'm on the road a lot."

"Enjoy it?"

"Sure. I wouldn't do it if I didn't. I think of myself as a modern troubadour . . . a sort of wandering minstrel from southeast Texas." She smiled at him, the lights of the dashboard catching the glittering blue of her eyes, this time, he sensed, telling the truth. "Given where you live, I gather you're a stick-in-the-mud Yankee?"

In spite of himself—in spite of Holly Paynter's lying, thieving ways—Julian laughed. "Too beautiful out there to leave, isn't it? Or have you been talking to my brother and sister? They think I'm fast becoming the town recluse."

"Nothing's too beautiful to leave once in a while. It always looks better when you come back. But I haven't been talking to anyone in Millbrook about you. I'm a pretty good reader of people, usually—I can spot a stick-in-the-mud when I see one."

He had no reason to doubt her. "Do you ever get tired of wandering?"

"I thought we were talking about you."

"I'm not sure we're talking about anything, just passing the time. Dare I ask where we're headed?"

She laughed, a delicious sound that filled him with an indescribable longing, and he had to restrain himself to keep from glancing back at the cot. "My, my," she said, clearly having fun. "Here I've admitted to borrowing the goblets and you still don't trust me."

"Borrowing? Stealing's more like it! Since when—"

"All in due time, all in due time."

Julian twitched in the patched, but comfortable, van seat. *Now she's setting me up*, he thought, *but for what?* The woman was relentless—and doubtlessly too damned captivating for his own good. Ever since she'd blinked plaster dust out of her eyes and fastened their sapphire beauty on him, he'd endured a slow-building fire inside him . . . a deep, primitive longing that had damned little to do with lies about puppies and names and goblets.

Grabbing her around the waist back at her room had nearly been his undoing. He'd acted on impulse, thinking more of ends than of means; he hadn't been about to let her march out on him. So he'd stopped her. Simple enough. Except the feel of her soft skin under the thin cotton of her robe had deposited a few more hot coals in the pit of his stomach. He was torturing himself, wanting this woman, knowing once would never be enough, that it would only make him want her more, again and again and again. Yet she was a wanderer. He might have her once, but then she'd be gone, back to her wandering. He wasn't going to set himself up for that kind of agony—or her. He didn't want her to change, not because of him and his "stick-in-the-mud" ways.

He willed away his contradictory thoughts—*make sense, will you?*—and watched her drive past Mill Brook Post and Beam, its lights glowing softly in the darkness of the riverbank.

"Whoops," she said, trod on the brakes, checked the rearview mirror for traffic and flipped her trusty van into reverse. "Kind of sneaks up on you, doesn't it?"

It didn't, especially when it was dark and its lights the first in a couple of miles. But he didn't say anything, smiling to himself as he imagined what might have been preoccupying her thoughts. Were there a few hot coals blazing inside her, distracting her from her thieving business? Or had she just been preoccupied with fine-tuning whatever lie she had in store for him?

The van hit a patch of ice in the parking area and skidded, and she stomped on the brake, way too hard. Before Julian could warn her, they were fishtailing and out of control. Holly didn't panic—but there wasn't a whole lot she could do. The van finally came to a wild, crooked stop inches from Adam's truck.

"Whoa," Holly said, collapsing back against her seat and breathing out a sigh.

Julian shook his head, unperturbed. "You learn after a while to take your foot off the brake in a skid. Just makes it worse if you stomp on the brake."

"I know that."

"You still did it."

"Goes against nature, not trying to stop when your vehicle's about to careen into a river."

"You're yards from the river."

"Whole yards, huh? Gee, that makes me feel so much better."

Julian laughed. "Rather deal with a hurricane, huh?"

"You bet."

"I'll make sure that spot gets sanded."

Holly yanked on the emergency brake and turned off the engine; he noticed a slight tremble in her hands as the lights went off. He couldn't blame her. As many uncontrollable skids as he'd been in, he was never prepared when one happened. All things considered, hers wasn't too bad—they'd never whipped completely around. But he doubted she'd appreciate such a distinction.

"You want me to hold your hand on the way in, keep you from slipping on the ice?" he asked.

"What makes you so sure I'll slip and you won't? As far as I can see, ice is ice and it doesn't matter if you live with it or not, if you hit it wrong, down you go." She looked at him, her lips pulled tightly together. "Besides, I'm not sure us holding hands is a good idea, you accusing me of thievery and all."

"You think I'd push you?" He could feel his eyes twinkling; he'd known just what she'd meant.

"No—never mind. Let's just get this over with."

She'd gotten herself so worked up, she jumped out of the van and obviously forgot about the ice. With a swear and a yell, down she went. Julian leaned over to make sure she hadn't hit her head, but she was already grabbing the open door and pulling herself up, cursing him, Yankees in general, snow, ice, New England winters and her own damned idiocy. By the time she finished, Julian had walked, more cautiously than he'd have ever admitted to her, around the van, spied a sanded spot and quickly occupied it.

She scowled at him. "You have something on your boots to keep you from slipping?"

"Nope. It is icy—"

"Well, thank you, sir, for telling me that. I don't think I could have figured it out for myself, just having nearly dunked us in the river and rebruised my back end and all.'

"Looks to me," he went on, "as if Abby and David have been trying to make themselves a skating rink again. Adam'll have a talk with them."

He put out a hand to help her, but she shook her head, which threw off her already precarious balance and her feet almost went out from under her again. But she recovered, with no help from him, and slipping and sliding, made her way to the sanded section near the walk.

IT'S FUN! IT'S FREE!
AND IT COULD MAKE YOU A
MILLIONAIRE

If you've ever played scratch-off lottery tickets, you should be familiar with how our games work. On each of the first four tickets (numbered 1 to 4 in the upper right)—there are PINK METALLIC STRIPS to scratch off.

Using a coin, do just that—carefully scratch the PINK STRIPS to reveal how much each ticket could be worth if it is a winning ticket. Tickets could be worth from $5.00 to $1,000,000.00 in lifetime money.

Note, also, that each of your 4 tickets has a unique sweepstakes Lucky Number...and that's 4 chances for a **BIG WIN!**

FREE BOOKS!

At the same time you play your tickets for big cash prizes, you are invited to play ticket #5 for the chance to get *one or more free books* from Harlequin. We give away free books to introduce readers to the benefits of the *Harlequin Reader Service®*

Accepting these free books places you under no obligation to buy anything! You may keep your free books and return your statement marked "cancel", and you will receive no more books. If you decide to keep them, every month we'll deliver 4 of the newest Harlequin Temptation® novels right to your door. You'll pay the low members-only price of just $2.39* each—a savings of 26 cents apiece off the cover price! And there's no charge for shipping and handling! You can cancel at any time simply by writing "cancel" on your statement or by returning a shipment of books to us at our cost.

PLUS...MORE FREE EXTRAS!

★ FREE GIFTS FROM TIME TO TIME!
★ FREE NEWSLETTER WITH AUTHOR PROFILES
   AND PREVIEWS!
★ FREE CONVENIENT HOME DELIVERY!

Of course, you may play "THE BIG WIN" without requesting any free books by scratching tickets #1 through #4 only. But remember, the first shipment of one or more books is FREE!

PLUS A FREE GIFT!

One more thing, when you accept the free book(s) on ticket #5 you are also entitled to play ticket #6 which is GOOD FOR A VALUABLE GIFT! Like the book(s) this gift is totally free and yours to keep as thanks for giving our Reader Service a try!

So scratch off the PINK STRIPS on all your BIG WIN tickets and send for everything today! You've got nothing to lose and everything to gain!

THE BIG WIN

Here are your BIG WIN Game Tickets, worth from $5.00 to $1,000,000.00 each. Scratch off the PINK METALLIC STRIP on each of your sweepstakes tickets to see what you could win and mail your entry right away. (See official rules in back of book for details!)

This could be your lucky day – GOOD LUCK!

FOLD AND DETACH ALONG THIS DOTTED LINE—RETURN ALL GAME TICKETS INTACT.

TICKET 1
Scratch PINK METALLIC STRIP to reveal potential value of this ticket if it is a winning ticket. Return all game tickets intact.
LUCKY NUMBER
5E438422

TICKET 2
Scratch PINK METALLIC STRIP to reveal potential value of this ticket if it is a winning ticket. Return all game tickets intact.
LUCKY NUMBER
1K436007

TICKET 3
Scratch PINK METALLIC STRIP to reveal potential value of this ticket if it is a winning ticket. Return all game tickets intact.
LUCKY NUMBER
2E435658

TICKET 4
Scratch PINK METALLIC STRIP to reveal potential value of this ticket if it is a winning ticket. Return all game tickets intact.
LUCKY NUMBER
4E438950

TICKET 5
FREE BOOKS
We're giving away brand new books to selected individuals. Scratch PINK METALLIC STRIP for number of free books you will receive.
AUTHORIZATION CODE
130107-742

TICKET 6
FREE GIFT
We have an outstanding added gift for you if you are accepting our free books. Scratch PINK METALLIC STRIP to reveal gift.
AUTHORIZATION CODE
130107-742

YES! Enter my Lucky Numbers in The BIG WIN Sweepstakes and tell me if I've won any cash prize. If PINK METALLIC STRIP is scratched off on ticket #5, I will also receive one or more FREE Harlequin Temptation® novels along with the FREE GIFT on ticket #6, as explained on the opposite page.   U-H-T-11/89 142 CIH MDV2

NAME _____

ADDRESS _____ APT. _____

CITY _____ STATE _____ ZIP _____

Offer limited to one per household and not valid to current Temptation subscribers.
© 1989 HARLEQUIN ENTERPRISES LTD.   Printed in Canada

Carefully
detach card
along dotted
lines and
mail today!
Play
all your
BIG WIN
tickets
and get
everything
you're
entitled to-
including
FREE BOOKS
and a
FREE GIFT!

NO POSTAGE
NECESSARY
IF MAILED
IN THE
UNITED STATES

BUSINESS REPLY MAIL
FIRST CLASS MAIL   PERMIT NO. 717   BUFFALO, NY

POSTAGE WILL BE PAID BY ADDRESSEE

HARLEQUIN READER SERVICE
THE BIG WIN SWEEPSTAKES

901 FUHRMANN BLVD
PO BOX 1867
BUFFALO NY 14240-9952

"When we were kids, we did stuff like this for fun," Julian said.

"That right there is why kids grow up."

"What did you do for fun, when you were a kid?"

Her expression, pleased in spite of herself, told him she'd heard the genuine curiosity in his voice. She grinned. "Played with rattlesnakes. Come on, let's go fetch a couple of goblets."

Mill Brook Post and Beam was getting ready to close for the day. Abby and David were off in a corner squabbling over a game of marbles while they waited for their father to gather his work for the evening. Beth waved at Julian and Holly from her computer, where she was immersed in one of her collection of computer games—her way of winding down before heading home. She would get so absorbed in what she was doing Julian was convinced the mill could burn down around her and she'd just gripe about losing the electricity. But for Holly Paynter, he observed, his one and only sister not only looked up and waved, but shut down her computer.

Holly waved back, looking cheerful and perfectly at ease. She might as well have been on her own turf. Julian watched in amazement at her audacity as she strode across the old pine flooring and started exchanging pleasantries with his sister.

With the two women preoccupied, Adam took the opportunity to look over and scowl at his younger brother. Adam Stiles hated lying to anybody, but to Holly Wingate Paynter, well-known storyteller, delightful woman, professionally interested in Millbrook and the mill—Julian knew his brother was squirming over what he'd done. Hell, he thought, Holly Paynter can lie to anybody but nobody can lie to her without feeling guilty.

"Come on, kids, let's go," Adam said. He grabbed his stack of work as his two children scrambled for their marbles, understanding that when their father said it was time to go, there was no arguing. On his way past Julian, he muttered, "You're lucky you're my brother. I don't like lying and I don't like setting people up."

"All in a noble cause, Adam," Julian said.

"Right. But maybe not the one you're thinking of."

"What's that supposed to mean?"

Adam gave his younger brother one of his rare half smiles. "All's fair in love and war, pal—only this ain't war, and if you're too stubborn to admit it, I'll just tell you myself."

"She's a thief—"

"So? Call the cops."

"Adam . . ."

"I know. That'd spoil the fun. You don't want my opinion, don't ask me to do asinine things. Now I'm off. I got a couple of hungry kids to feed."

Julian wasn't sorry to see him go. His older brother was scrupulously aboveboard in everything he did, including telling Julian exactly what was on his mind— no matter how uncomfortable it made him feel.

But he had another problem to deal with, namely his sister. "Julian, you big jerk," she hollered, marching his way. "Do you *always* have to jump to negative conclusions about people?"

Sometimes he didn't know why he didn't move to Seattle. He glared at Holly, smirking as she followed

Beth across to the reception area. "What have you been telling my sister?"

"My woes," Holly said innocently, her eyes glittering.

"*I've* got the damned goblets," Beth interrupted. "Holly gave them to me after she swiped them from your place. They're over on my desk. Take them, for God's sake."

He just stood there, blinking like a damned fool. "What?"

Beth huffed, indignant. "It was *supposed* to be a surprise."

Julian tried to look as if he was expecting this curve, but he wasn't a professional storyteller. He figured he just looked as if he'd been had.

"I've decided to do a storytelling performance while I'm here in Millbrook," Holly said.

Beth took over eagerly. "At Holly's suggestion, we're organizing a fund-raising benefit for the historical society. It'll be a week from today. Holly's donating her time. Can you believe our good fortune?"

"When did Holly make this suggestion?"

"This afternoon," Beth said.

"Right." Another story. Julian recovered fast, although he knew it was probably too late: he'd been had again. "What's this got to do with the goblets?"

"I snuck them out of your house," Holly said, "to show your sister and discuss the idea of using them as a prop in my performance. I was going to tell you about it and return them, of course."

"Of course."

"But first I needed some advice from someone who knows Millbrook and whom I felt I could trust."

"Namely me," Beth supplied proudly—and with a scathing look at her notoriously skeptical brother. "Holly's a *Wingate*"

"That's right," Holly agreed, blithely lying through her previous lie about that subject. "As I explained to you, Julian, I came to Millbrook because of the goblets. What I didn't tell you—again, so as not to ruin my surprise—was that I'm distantly related to Zachariah Wingate. That further attracted me to the story of the goblets, the scandal, the idea of their being buried in an old New England dirt cellar."

Beth nodded, swallowing every word. "Ever since she arrived in Millbrook, she'd been toying with the idea of surprising us by working up a preliminary story involving the goblets and the Scandal of 1889—and premiering it in a fund-raiser for the historical society."

"Ah-ha," Julian remarked.

"And *you*, you cynical SOB," Beth went on, referring to the younger of her two brothers, "had to accuse her of stealing the goblets!"

"She *did* steal the goblets."

Beth groaned. "She was just *borrowing* them! Oh, Julian, for heaven's sake, don't be so mean minded. You should have been able to look at Holly, realize what her reputation is and given her the benefit of the doubt. Now—well, *I've* apologized for you on behalf of Millbrook, for having the likes of you living around here, but I think you should apologize on your own behalf."

If Beth hadn't been a hothead since she was six months old, her outburst might have irritated Julian, but he understood his only sister. And he was beginning to understand Holly Paynter: she *always* had a contingency plan.

"An apology from Julian's not necessary," she said, sounding so pure. "Really. I'm just glad we got this straightened out before the police got involved."

Beth was having none of it. "Well, *I* think he owes you one."

Two can play this game, Julian thought. He smiled, as if he meant it, and gave Holly a mock-bow. If his sister hadn't been standing there watching, he'd have kissed her—but their next kiss, he thought, wasn't going to be one he'd want to have his sister around for. "My sincere apologies for having misjudged you, Ms Paynter," he said. "Now you can let me make amends by permitting me to take you to dinner—"

"That's more like it," Beth muttered, turning to her new friend from Texas.

Holly's only graceful choice was to remain innocent looking, smile and accept.

HOLLY KEPT HER EYES pinned to the winding road, not driving recklessly, but a little too fast. She could feel Julian's dark gaze on her. He hadn't said a word. No arguments, no accusations, no demands. Not a *sound*. It was unsettling.

She wondered what she'd gotten herself into this time. Grandpa Wingate would be sighing and shaking his head, reserving comment on her big mouth, her impatience and her stubborn ways.

The Windham House was brightly lit against the sharp, clear evening sky. Holly pulled into the parking area next to Julian's Land Rover, a dirt-spattered hulk next to the skiers' trim BMWs and Grand Prixs. The man was solid. Down-to-earth.

And playing games with her over a couple of very valuable sterling-silver goblets. Millbrook, Vermont, she'd warned herself, was something to be survived—and Julian Stiles was a part of that picturesque, but treacherous, New England town.

She'd never been so glad for a gust of cold air as when she climbed out of her van and took a deep, refreshing breath.

"I'm not hungry after all this hullabaloo over those goblets," she said as he came round the van and stood next to her. "It's six o'clock. I need to check in with my answering service in Houston and do some work. Then I think I'll just crash."

Julian leaned back against the van, oblivious to the film of road sand and salt eating away at her paint job. New England was as hard on cars as it was on people, she thought.

"You just want to get away from me," he said in a low, gravelly voice.

She shrugged. "I could grit out dinner with you if I had to, but—"

"You'd rather dine with an alligator," he finished for her, smiling.

"Julian Stiles, you don't scare me a lick. I hope you know that."

"I'm not trying to scare you."

"But you could if you tried? You sound like the playground bully. Forget dinner, all right? And don't read anything into my refusal. Let's just leave it that I'm not hungry."

"Chortling'll make you lose your appetite."

"Who's chortling?"

"You are. You've been chortling since we left the mill."

"I most certainly have not. I never made a sound!"

"Didn't need to. Inside you're chortling—gloating because you think you got the best of me with this latest lie of yours. Doesn't your stomach hurt from trying to keep from laughing? That's why you don't want to eat."

Her stomach *had* hurt for a little while, at first from repressed laughter, then from the tension of his continued silence. It felt better now that he was jousting with her again. With any other man, she would have given up on the Paul Revere goblets and accepted what Great-grandfather Zachariah had been forced to accept a hundred years ago: with the Danvers-Stiles crowd, a Wingate was doomed. Common sense told her to cut her losses, never mind the damned goblets and get out of Millbrook. But common sense wasn't fun or challenging. It was generally dull and safe.

"Look, Julian," she said reasonably, "I can understand you're probably embarrassed by what happened—"

He laughed softly, incredulously. "Wrong, sweetheart. I don't embarrass easily."

The word "sweetheart" sent warm, liquid sensations up her back. "Um . . ." She wasn't one to hem and haw once she'd gotten started, but she hadn't expected him to sound so self-controlled. As if she'd only done exactly what he'd *expected* her to do. *Oh dear.* She inhaled. "Still, you did jump to conclusions about me, and setting you right was as difficult for me as it must have been for you. Maybe more difficult."

He shifted his weight, bending one knee as he crossed his arms on his chest. "An elaborate lie like that wears thin, does it?"

She pursed her lips. "You can be really obnoxious, you know that? Here I am, just trying to do what I do best—"

"Tell stories."

"That's right." She wasn't going to let him ruffle her. "I wanted my visit to Millbrook to be extra special. Don't ask me why because I'm not even sure I know, but when I saw that piece on the goblets—something happened to me. I just knew I had to come to Millbrook . . . and, I don't know. I guess I've been acting a little crazy ever since. I'm creative, but I'm also a professional. I've never done anything like what I did today, and all for a surprise. And an uncertain one at that. I wasn't sure the historical society would even go for my fund-raising night idea."

Julian shook his head, not believing much of anything she said. "All to pull your behind out of the fire."

Never had she met a man who could see through her defenses with such natural ease. "Believe whatever you want to believe. It makes no difference to me. Now if you'll excuse me, I'm getting cold."

"I'm not going to let the goblets out of my sight."

"Fine," she said coolly, "don't."

He touched her upper arm. "Or you."

"Julian . . ." She didn't pull back.

"Something's going on between us," he said softly, moving close enough that all she had to do was lean forward ever so slightly and she could rest her forehead on his shoulder; she resisted. "I just don't know where it's going to lead."

She wanted to answer—wanted to tell him there was nothing going on between them, nothing that was going to lead anywhere, good, bad or indifferent. But nothing came out. She could feel her mouth tingle in anticipation; he must have sensed her desire. He sighed, not with disgust but simple surrender, and kissed her, so lightly, just his lips brushing hers.

"Have a pleasant evening," he said, his eyes suddenly dancing.

"You, too."

As she started up the flagstone path toward the Windham House, she sensed Julian watching her from his position against her van. Heat seemed to radiate from his gaze—raw, masculine desire. She kept sucking in the cold evening air, hoping to counter the effect he was having on her. She wished the kiss had gone on longer.

"Holly."

His voice was low and sandpapery. She slowed her pace, but didn't stop. If she did, she might never make it back into the cheerful, welcoming Windham House.

"I know you're planning something," he went on. "Just don't count on getting away with the goblets or on doing anything to cheat my family or anyone else in Millbrook."

She glanced over her shoulder and clicked her tongue against the roof of her mouth, almost glad that he was back to issuing orders and demands—challenges. "Such a cynic you are."

His tone didn't change, but she could see him willing back a grudging smile on his smug, handsome Yankee face. The man knew just what he was doing.

"Won't matter where you slither off to," he said, his tone idle, almost teasing, just daring her, "I'll find you."

"Slither?" That got her, elitist Danvers-Stiles that he was. "*Slither!* Are you accusing me of being a snake in the grass? Because I'll have you know—"

"Try anything before you leave town and I'll track you down."

She tried to match his calm, but his choice of verb—*slither*, for heaven's sake—still rankled. So she opted for sarcasm. "I can count on that, can I?"

His smile was less grudging, filled with confidence and self-control, and admiration, she thought. She wasn't having any more effect on controlling his actions than he was on controlling hers. "You bet."

"I'll keep that in mind," she said, whirling back around. She would, too. "But tracking me down might not be as easy as you think."

He couldn't have heard her, but he called from the darkness behind her, "Don't think I won't find you, because I will."

He might try, she thought, but was even a Danvers-Stiles that persistent? Wandering minstrel that she was, she didn't keep an ordinary schedule, if she kept one at all. But she didn't want to underestimate any descendant of the men who'd drummed her great-grandfather out of town. Maybe Julian would put himself to the task and . . .

Lordy, woman, do you want him to find you once you're shed of this place?

She shivered at the ramifications of the question, refused to answer it and ran inside. Only when she was warming herself by the fire did the full impact of the last hour or so hit her. And it hit her hard.

If she stuck to the "tale" she'd told Julian and Beth Stiles and went ahead with giving a performance at the hastily arranged Millbrook Historical Society fundraiser, she'd have to spend another week in one place. And not just in any old one place, but in *Millbrook*.

What couldn't Julian Stiles worm out of her in one whole week?

She'd planned to leave town Sunday afternoon—if not sooner. Planned to leave with the goblets, with no one the wiser about what she'd done or who she was. Now all Millbrook would know she was Holly Paynter, the storyteller, and she was going to have to put together a story about the goblet scandal of 1889.

What a tangle of lies and half-truths she'd woven!

And all for the goblets and family pride?

No, she thought. Not all. They'd gotten her to Millbrook, but they weren't what was keeping her there.

Julian Danvers Stiles was, and that, she thought, might be the scariest part of all.

7

"THIS IS VERY EMBARRASSING," Dorothy Windham said over Sunday afternoon tea. Just she and Holly were in the parlor. She set her cup and saucer on her lap and stared out at an oriole prancing among her bird feeders.

Holly didn't want to make the older woman feel awkward, but Dorothy's news had knocked her further off balance. She hadn't quite gotten her bearings in Millbrook since crashing through the Danvers House ceiling and was despairing she ever would.

Now this.

"You're booked up for the entire week?"

Dorothy nodded painfully. "I feel terrible about it, particularly since you've volunteered your time and talent for the historical society."

"You shouldn't feel bad," Holly said, wishing she could make herself sound more sincere. The truth was, however, that without the Windham House, she didn't know where she'd stay. Ordinarily she'd just camp out in her van, but the mercury had dipped close to zero last night. Vermont in late January was no place to camp. What was she supposed to do? *You could always go back to Florida where you belong.* Florida, of course, wasn't home, and she wasn't at all sure it was where she belonged. But clearly she *didn't* belong in southern Vermont.

"My nephew Julian proposed a solution you might consider," her hostess said hopefully.

Holly tried not to look too skeptical. She'd had a feeling Julian's hand had been stirring this particular stinking pot. Sipping tea, she asked noncommittally, "What's that?"

"He made the point—and I quite agree—that since you're offering your services on Millbrook's behalf, you shouldn't have to pay for your lodgings here."

"Mrs. Windham, you don't owe me a free room . . ."

"I do, and if I had a spare one to give you, I certainly wouldn't charge you. I've been a member of the Millbrook Historical Society for forty years, and I'll be the first to say that we could never have afforded to pay you for what you've so generously agreed to give us. I might also add that word of your performance has begun to circulate and it's sure to be a sellout. No, I'm in complete agreement with Julian that we should find you a place to stay here in town."

Holly shook her head. "I won't impose on strangers."

"Julian thought you might feel that way, but he was hoping you wouldn't consider him a stranger."

"Him?"

"Yes, he's offered to take you in as his guest."

It was all Holly could do to keep from choking on her tea. "I've been out to his house—"

"Lovely, isn't it? You could really absorb the atmosphere of a New England winter out there. Holly, I wouldn't even bring up such an invitation if I didn't know my nephew. He's a sweet, gentle, thoughtful young man."

He's a sneaky bastard is what he is, Holly thought. Sending his aunt in to do the dirty work. No room at the inn, no place to go but out into the woods with that wolf. Hell, no she'd rather leave town now!

Then Grandpa Wingate's voice came to her. It was filled with regret—and repressed anger. She could feel the heat and humidity of that summer night on the Gulf, when it was just the two of them together in their tiny house.

"Wasn't a week went by that my daddy didn't tell me about how bad he felt, not having those goblets to pass on to me, and me to your mother, and her to you. He'd have liked you, Holly. He'd have liked your spunk. He never forgave himself for losing the goblets. Felt he let all of us future Wingates down."

How could she think of leaving Millbrook without the goblets? They didn't belong to Julian. They weren't his to protect.

But she forced herself to recall the rest of her grandfather's words, spoken so many times over the years.

"Pride drove your great-grandpa to try to donate those goblets to that darned academy. You never forget that, Holly, y'hear? Don't you ever let your pride get in the way of your good judgment, lest you do something stupid and people accuse you of things you never did and never meant to happen."

They were words to remember.

And yet her grandfather had never met Julian Stiles and if she snuck off now . . .

She poised her teacup midair and froze. The thought was there, formed and complete.

If she snuck off now, not only would she not have the goblets, but she'd never see Julian again.

But if she waited, bided her time, plotted and schemed and got the goblets back—and *then* if she left town, with the goblets...

Julian would track her down. He'd said so.

"Lordy," she muttered under her breath, "you really are nuts."

Setting down her tea and reaching for a piping hot applesauce-oatmeal muffin, Holly told Dorothy Windham she'd be happy to discuss staying with her nephew.

Even if, she added silently, it was the most outrageous thing she'd ever done.

HOLLY LISTENED to dire warnings of a "nor'easter" on her van radio as she bumped along Julian's impossible driveway. The forecast called for ten to twelve inches of snow. She shivered at the prospect. She and Julian could shovel snow together. Break their backs and then collapse by the fire. How invigorating.

You could give him a back rub...

If she threw her van into reverse and backed out now, she might make Virginia before the snowstorm hit. But she no longer could pretend that was an option. If not for the goblets, if not for whatever was going on between her and Julian, she still had to stay. Her own professional reputation was involved now. She had agreed to do a fund-raiser for the Millbrook Historical Society. It was a commitment. She needed to keep it.

At last, Julian's house came into view. He'd left the outside light on for her, given winter's early sundowns. It wasn't even dinnertime and already dark, still darker out in the woods. Holly parked and got out her leather satchel, hastily but expertly packed. Dorothy Windham had given her a paper sack of sweet rolls to take up to her nephew; Holly grabbed them, too. She acknowledged her pulse was racing, and she wasn't quite sure what the devil she was doing or why, just that she was going to go ahead and stay out here in the wilderness. With Julian Stiles. It'd be just the two of them.

And his dogs.

And her imagination.

"The man works," she reminded herself. "And so do you: you've got a story to concoct."

She knocked and let herself in. Julian was busy setting the table in the dining area, his hair still damp from a recent shower. She smiled at him from the kitchen and set the sweet rolls on the counter and her satchel at her feet. The rush of awkwardness she'd anticipated feeling didn't materialize. Instead her frayed nerves relaxed at the smell of baking apples and the melodic, rasping sounds of Mose Allison on the stereo.

"Hey, there," Julian said, smiling at her as he set out two wineglasses. "Welcome."

"You sound sincere."

He laughed. "I'm always sincere."

"Julian, why did you do this?"

"Because I'm a thoughtful nephew who wanted to get his aunt out of an embarrassing situation."

"It's hardly her fault—"

"I know that and you know that, but Aunt Doe is a very gracious woman."

"And you want to keep an eye on me."

He came into the kitchen. "That I do."

"I appreciate your honesty," she said.

"Why did you come?"

She shrugged. "Because it was easier than not coming."

"You're not madly curious about how I live?"

"I've seen how you live."

"But," he said, leaning against an oak counter, "you haven't experienced it. Maybe you'll come to understand why I love it out here so much. Would you like me to carry your bag upstairs?"

"No, I'll do it. I . . . um . . . hope I'm not putting you out."

"Not at all." He pointed into the living room. "Stairs are right back there."

They led to a cozy loft with wood floors, wood walls, a slanted wood ceiling and railing overlooking the cathedral-ceilinged living room below. Holly could easily imagine Julian and his brother and sister cutting the wood for the huge beams. She set her satchel on the double platform bed. There was just one. And obviously this was the only bedroom. She was perfectly aware of the sexual tension between her and the Yankee downstairs, but she wasn't certain she wanted to act on it just yet, with all that remained unresolved between them. And she damned well knew she didn't appreciate his being that matter-of-fact about it. Just having her dump her things upstairs in his bedroom didn't strike her as particularly sexy or romantic—not that she planned to tell *him* that.

There was always that chance she was jumping to conclusions.

She popped her head over the railing and called down, "You sure you don't mind me using your bed?"

"Nope," he said from the kitchen.

Of course he wouldn't if he planned to share it with her. Bad phrasing of a question. She tried again. "I hate to put you out of your own bedroom."

He ambled into the living room and looked up at her, slowly wiping a knife with a dish towel. He grinned. "Holly," he said, "you don't have to fret. The couch pulls out."

"Oh. I just didn't want you to have to sleep on the floor."

Before her cheeks could flush crimson—not from embarrassment, but from *awareness*—she pulled her head back from over the railing. Even with him downstairs on the couch, it was going to be close quarters.

Which maybe was the whole idea behind his invitation.

Dinner was roast turkey breast, baby carrots, salad, French bread and baked apples. Julian explained he was a decent basic cook but left the gourmet recipes to his friends who were starting up the Silver Goblets Restaurant. They were going to be out later in the week; perhaps they could cook a meal for them.

"Every time they cook here, though," he said, "they destroy my kitchen—but all in a good cause."

"How's work on the Danvers House going?" Holly refused to call it the Silver Goblets Restaurant; it demeaned her great-grandfather.

"Slowly. I've decided to bring in outside help or we'll never get the place done. I have just so much time with work at the sawmill, that place and chasing you around."

She pursed her lips. "You don't have to chase me."

He regarded her over the rim of his wineglass. "Maybe I want to."

"How long have you lived out here?"

"Change the subject, huh? Okay. About ten years."

"Always alone?"

"More or less."

"Then you've never married?"

He grinned at her blunt question. "Is this a story-teller's curiosity at work?"

"I suppose. What else could it be?"

"I'll spare you this time and not answer that. No, I've never been married. I came close once—about the time I was building this place, as a matter of fact. Fortunately I figured out before the wedding date that Isabel's main attraction to me was the challenge of trying to reform and 'tame' me. Being a Stiles and a Danvers and an alumnus of both Millbrook Academy and Williams College, I was supposed to exhibit a certain 'refinement' that she considered lacking in me. But I am what I am."

"Aren't we all? Did she specify what she intended to reform?"

"I was supposed to give up living in the woods, move to a big white house with black shutters on Old Mill-

brook Common and establish myself as the 'brains' of
Mill Brook Post and Beam and make Adam stick to the
'brawn.'"

"Adam doesn't strike me as being a dummy," Holly
said.

"He's not."

"And I don't think you're lacking in the brawn
department, either."

"Why, thank you."

"I've never gone in for the idea that a woman's job is
to change a man—or vice versa. Falling in love can
change people's lives, obviously, but to go into it with
specific goals in mind—with a list, for heaven's sake.
That strikes me as pretty arrogant. And I don't see men
as *necessarily* wild and untamed creatures, do you?
Anyway, I wouldn't fall in love with one that was."

"Who would you fall in love with?" he asked huskily.

"If I had a shopping list of qualities for the man I
want, I'd be as bad as the woman who takes any man
and tries to mold him into her image of the perfect man.
That doesn't interest me. I'm more interested in getting
to know people as they are, letting change occur nat-
urally, not forcing it. If I fall in love, I fall in love. If I
don't—I have a pretty full life."

He leaned back in his chair across from her, the night-
darkened woods through the undraped windows serving as a backdrop. "That strikes me as solid thinking."

"Solid thinking and one's emotions don't always go
hand in hand." *Take you, for example,* she thought.
*Solid thinking tells me I shouldn't be within miles of
here—but where am I?*

"How true," he said.

"It's easy to get involved with someone whose life-style and attitudes don't blend with yours and never will. I had a relationship with a guy once—way back when—whose idea of my being a storyteller was that I'd tell bedtime stories to a half-dozen of our wee bumpkins to send them off to dreamland."

Julian added more wine to her glass, then to his. "He didn't see you as a professional?"

"I work weird hours, I'm on the road a lot and in those days I wasn't earning much money. It looked like a nice hobby to him. Storytelling's not the most certain profession in the world. But I was making my own way, and I had ideas about where I wanted to go with my career—which, by the way, is pretty much where I am now. He just assumed I wasn't all that serious."

"That would be irritating, I'm sure." Julian drank some wine; the Mose Allison tape had ended, leaving the house in that all-encompassing silence. "What about children—you're not interested in having any?"

"No, I am. And I'd love to tell them bedtime stories. But I don't like having my life dictated to me. I need to figure things out for myself, especially about my work—it's such a part of who I am."

"That's fairly obvious," he said, and she wasn't sure if he was referring to her tales about lost puppies and whatnot or if he was beginning to see her for who she was.

She went on quickly, "Of course, that doesn't mean there isn't room for compromise and change."

"Both of which can be painful."

"In the short term, maybe. I think change always hurts in a way. That doesn't automatically make it bad.

If you get too stuck in your ways, you turn to stone. You get mean. Bored."

Julian smiled, somewhat skeptically. "From what I gather, you're never in one place long enough to get stuck in any particular way."

"Maybe wandering's the way I'm stuck in," she said, getting up with her wine and going over to the fire. "When I was little my father was in the military and we moved all around. Then my mother died when I was ten and we moved around some more, just the two of us, drifting. My Grandpa Wingate got sick of me getting carted from one place to another, so I ended up going to live with him. My father got a job on an oil rig and was gone for long periods—I just stayed with Grandpa."

"Where's your father now?"

"Still in Texas. He retires in a couple of years. He's got a woman friend now, someone who understands him— someone *he* understands. They just let each other be. Grandpa died five years ago. I guess I'll always miss him."

Julian brought out the baked apples, and they ate them sitting on the floor by the fire. The dogs had better manners than to beg.

"You're an intriguing woman," Julian said. "I'm not going to pretend otherwise."

She grinned at him. "But?"

"But I don't know what the hell you're up to."

"Ask me."

"No way. I'm not putting you on the spot. Whenever I apply a little pressure, your imagination clicks into high gear. I don't want any more stories. You can tell me what's going on when you're ready."

"Julian . . ."

"Don't, Holly. No protests. I told you: no pressure. You're a guest in my house. It's not polite for me to make you lie—and don't tell me you haven't lied because you know damn well you have. So let's just call a truce for now."

She sighed. "All right, but I'd argue your assumptions."

"You'd argue anything, I do believe."

Only with a Danvers-Stiles. "I'll just leave it at that. If you don't object, I've got a few things I'd like to do, so I'll just go on upstairs. Is there anything you need?"

He looked at her, but his expression was unreadable. "Nothing I can't get in the morning."

"Thanks for dinner."

"You're welcome," he said, and she could feel him watching her as she headed upstairs. It was just nine o'clock, but she didn't know what else to do. Play cards? Put on more Mose Allison? The truth was, she wasn't ready to talk openly. Julian Stiles seemed to be fishing around, half jousting with her, half toying with an offer of friendship. In a way, she would have liked to have everything out in the open, but that seemed too risky. He could just boot her out. She could hardly blame him if he wanted to. Or he could tell her he agreed with her, could appreciate her claim to the goblets and the "tales" that had resulted because of it. And then what?

Better to keep Julian guessing.

It was not a way of managing him, she admitted, but of keeping him alert and interested. Of keeping him on her tail.

An honest, heart-to-heart talk with the man could spell the end to the elusive, tenuous relationship they had. For now, it was safer just to keep things as they were.

But frustrating.

She popped her head over the railing and told him she'd sit up and read for a while, then hit the sack.

"Let me know," he said, looking from his position in front of the fire, "if you need more blankets."

Yeah, right. Then he could come upstairs and tuck her in.

The thought was enough to make her hardly notice how frigid the sheets were when she climbed into bed.

THE HOWLING WIND and the sounds of snow smacking up against the windows woke Holly from a troubled sleep. She inhaled sharply at the shock of not knowing where she was. But she held the breath, not letting it come out in a panicked cry, as her eyes adjusted to the darkness and she could make out the sturdy, pleasant lines of Julian's loft bedroom.

She listened for his breathing. Would he snore?

But she heard only the wind, and finally, unable to roll over and go back to sleep, she crept out from under his down comforter and peered over the railing.

There was no light on downstairs, but she could make out his silhouette in the window, looking out at the snowy, predawn landscape. He gave no indication he was aware of her presence. Her heart pounded; it was a wonder he couldn't hear it. She wanted to say something—to go to him.

He seemed so very alone.

Yet if she padded downstairs now, she knew they would come back up together. They would make love. The snow, the wind, the isolation and silence of the place—they'd all have their effect. It would seem as if the rest of the world, the goblets, the lies, the impossibility of a wanderer and a mountain man loner having any future together, didn't matter. They would have to wake up in the cold light of dawn and realize those things did matter, that their isolation was only temporary, and no escape. Would it make a difference, though, if they woke up in each other's arms?

You're tired, she told herself. *Dreaming.*

Or just too damned cautious.

She started to call down to him, started to tiptoe over to the stairs. But she stopped herself, slipping back to bed, under the covers where it wasn't as warm as she remembered on awakening.

After a while, she heard his footfall and his deep sigh as he lowered himself onto the couch, and she wondered if he went to sleep right away, or lay awake, thinking, as long as she did.

Her sanity returned with morning. Scrambling out of bed, she all but collapsed with relief that she had resisted tempting Julian's hormones last night—not to mention her own. She had enough troubles as it was. She peeked over the railing and saw he'd vacated the couch. In other words, the coast was clear. She trotted downstairs.

"Wow," she said, going to the windows in the dining area, "look at that snow."

That was precisely what Julian was doing. He was in jeans, but his flannel shirt was untucked and he wasn't wearing shoes. There was something disconcertingly sexy about a man in stocking feet. His hair was tousled, his square jaw unshaved. He looked as if he'd passed a bad night.

"It's still coming down," he pointed out, unnecessarily.

"How many inches would you say it's snowed already? I didn't notice how much was on the ground to begin with."

"Eight inches at least. I'd say we'll get a good twelve, fourteen by the time the storm's finished." He glanced at her, taking in the men's red flannel nightshirt she'd picked up for her stay in New England. It was toasty warm and distinctly unsexy. "That's quite a getup."

"It's warm."

"I'll bet. You don't look as if you're in a hurry to get anywhere."

"I'm not, but don't you have to be at the sawmill?"

He shrugged, unconcerned. "It's Monday morning. I've got some calls to make, but I can do that from here. Everything else can wait. Adam'll gripe about it, but he and Beth can cover for me. I do it for him whenever one of the kids is sick. I'd cover for Beth anytime she wants, but she's as bad a workaholic as Adam. She just won't admit it."

"You're not as driven?"

"I'm not as single-minded about the sawmill. Buying the academy was my idea, for instance—and it's going to eat up a hell of a lot of my time. I've just never been your basic nine-to-five type."

"That I can relate to," she said. "So you'll go in late?"

"If at all."

She licked her lips at the prospect of being snowbound with him for the day. "Aren't you going to plow?"

"When the snow stops," he said, eyeing her with amusement.

"But that might not be for hours."

"Might not."

"Julian!"

He laughed. "Don't look so trapped. We'll have fun." He draped an arm over her shoulder, brotherlike. "Tell me, Holly Wingate Paynter of Houston, Texas, have you ever shoveled a foot of snow?"

8

LUCKY HER—Julian had two shovels. They went out after their bowls of oatmeal—they were saving the sweet rolls—and tackled the steps, the walks and the area in front of the garage. It was fine, powdery snow, no good for making snowballs. But Holly tried anyway. When she emptied her shovel, the wind would blow the snow back into her face, which never seemed to happen to Julian. He also never seemed to get snow down his neck or up his sleeves. He had given her gum shoes one look and shaken his head, but she'd worn two pairs of socks and her feet were doing all right.

She figured they'd shovel for a little while, then go inside for coffee and sweet rolls.

That wasn't how Julian figured it. Once he got started, he had to finish. It made sense to wait until the snow had stopped to plow, he explained, but shoveling you could keep at right through the storm; it was easier on the back. So he wanted to get everything shoveled this time out, and he'd come back later and shovel the last few inches from the storm. It was a sensible enough idea. It just took forever to accomplish.

At least to Holly.

"The snow's light, and despite your inexperience doing this kind of work, your help makes a difference," Julian told her. "This is going pretty quick."

She'd hate to be around for wet, heavy snow.

He caught her catching snowflakes on her tongue. "It's easier to drink a glass of water."

"That's not nearly as romantic."

"I don't know what's romantic about eating snow," he said.

The man was impossible. She got back to work.

"Hope I don't turn into an ice block before we get this job done," she muttered.

"If you do," he said, very close behind her, "I promise I'll take care to warm you up slowly."

Imagining countless scenarios of being warmed up by one Julian Danvers Stiles, Holly warned herself that drops in body temperature could bring on muddled thinking. She had no business imagining anything but where to dump her next shovelful of snow.

She couldn't resist.

He was standing in front of her, so businesslike, so Yankee smug and efficient with his shovel and watch cap and leather gloves and L.L. Bean boots. Snow was just snow to him.

"What the hell."

Just as he bent down to tackle another virgin area, Holly gave her shovel a well-practiced jerk and watched the heap of snow fly over his strong, solid back.

He yelled something that sounded rather uncensored to her and whipped around with a murderous look. Snow had blown onto his face and clung to his eyebrows.

"Whoops," she said, laughing. "My arms are getting weak from all this hefting. I couldn't control the shovel."

"You lying little . . ."

She didn't stick around for the rest, but dived back toward the house. Mountain man that he was, he caught up with her in no time. He grabbed her around the middle and hauled her into a deep drift near the kitchen window.

"Julian, don't you dare. I've never been in snow this deep."

He ignored her protests and heave-hoed her into the drift. She landed on her back, surprised at the snow's softness, the way it cushioned her fall. Relaxing, she spread-eagled and laughed up at him. He was breathing hard, laughing with her.

"Have you ever made a snow angel?" he asked.

"Nope."

"I'll show you."

He dropped onto his back into an untouched area of snow and, with his arms straight, brought them from his hips up and out over his head and back down, making angel wings. Keeping his legs straight, he brought them out to the sides, making the base of the angel. Holly sat up, watching in amazement. He looked like a little kid.

"There," he said, standing.

In the snow was the impression of one man-sized angel. Holly found herself a spot and dropped carefully, imitating his movements. If not for the cold wind and the snow in her face, she could have lain there all day, it was so comfortable.

Her angel was a little lopsided, but definitely recognizable. Holly was pleased with the results.

"Are you cold?"

"Freezing—but I'm sweating, too. Doesn't make sense."

Magnanimously, he agreed that they could go inside. They peeled off their snowy outer clothes and hung them on a long Shaker pegboard in the entry.

"Your cheeks are rosy," Holly told him.

He tapped her cheek with one knuckle. "So are yours."

She started to put on a kettle, but he shooed her out of the kitchen, handing her an afghan. "You're not used to this kind of weather—you'd better get warmed up."

Wrapping up in the heavy afghan, she sat by the fire while he stirred the blazing red coals and added another hunk of wood. Then he muttered something about heating up some cider and went into the kitchen. Holly poked her stockinged feet close to the flames. She could hear Julian opening the kitchen door, and in a moment the two dogs were brushing their icy fur against her, trying to take her spot in front of the fire. Julian called them off with an unintelligible growl, but they seemed to understand. They gave her some room.

In a few minutes, Julian returned with two mugs of steaming cider, handing her one as he wriggled in between her and Pen, who promptly flopped her head on his lap. He seemed hardly to notice. Holly cupped the mug, feeling its warmth on her near-frostbitten fingers.

"Warming up?" Julian asked.

"Getting there. Now that I'm thawing, I realize how cold I was getting. Mmm—this smells wonderful."

He settled down beside her, not touching her afghan. "Every fall, I take Abby and David apple picking, and we come back here and make up a batch of our own cider. We always think it's the best cider we've ever had."

Holly smiled, envisioning Vermont in autumn, Julian with his sleeves rolled up to his elbows as he raked leaves, his niece and nephew leaping into the brightly-colored piles. It was probably a hopelessly romanticized vision, but maybe trying to see life through her rose-colored glasses was one reason she was a storyteller...another being that she *knew* life wasn't like that. She was a Wingate, after all.

"Your niece and nephew seem to think a great deal of you," she said.

Julian shrugged. "They take me for who I am."

"And who are you?"

"What you see," he said, looking at her with those incredibly vivid eyes, "is what you get."

"Are you implying that's not the case with me?"

"Not necessarily. When you peel away all the defensive layers and finally come to the core Holly Paynter, I'll bet what you see is what you get. It's all those layers that give you pause, make you wonder."

She tried the cider, felt its warmth all the way down to her stomach. "Sort of like an artichoke, huh? I've never thought of myself that way."

He laughed softly, leaning back on one elbow, his eyes never leaving her. "Somehow when I look at you, I don't think artichoke. How's the cider?"

"Good—hot. It has cinnamon in it?"

"A little. I don't like to overpower good cider with too many spices."

"Can't blame you."

"Holly..."

"I'm just about warm."

"Good. You look antsy."

She forced herself to look away, into the crackling fire. "You know me—I get stir-crazy."

"Why is that?"

"It's my nature."

She could sense that he hadn't moved, was still studying her with those narrowed, insistent emerald eyes. Not giving up, he said, "There has to be more reason than that."

There was nothing demanding in his tone, but she whipped her head around, nearly spilling her cider. "Why should I tell you anything?"

"Because I'd like to know more about you," he said, unperturbed. "Because I care about you, Holly."

"I thought I was a lying Texan."

He smiled, amused. "And a thieving Wingate, don't forget."

"That's just coincidence." Unexpectedly this time the half-truth hurt; she almost winced.

"Layers, Holly. Just layers. I haven't gotten to the real you yet."

"Maybe I'm like an onion and you just keep peeling and peeling and all there is is more onion and more onion until finally you come to this hard little knot of a core that you throw away." She turned back to the fire. "Maybe that's me."

"How far are you going to carry these vegetable analogies? First you're an artichoke, now an onion. Next you'll be... I don't know, maybe a pineapple. Prickly on the outside, soft and sweet on the inside."

He was teasing her and she couldn't help but laugh, and not take herself—or him—so seriously. "You're not easily put off, are you?"

"Just a hardheaded Yankee."

"Okay. What do you want to know about me?"

He straightened up, putting his mug down, and with one finger turned her chin toward him. "Everything."

She wanted to say something, maybe even tried to, but all she could hear were the popping sounds of the fire, the deep, steady breathing of the dogs. Was there any place more peaceful than right here? *Let it snow all day...*

She didn't resist, didn't say a word, when Julian took her mug and set it on the hearth, out of the way.

"My brother thinks we're playing hands-off games," he said quietly, "especially me."

"What do you think?"

"Maybe he had a point."

"Had," she repeated.

"You got it."

And he brushed his mouth, so soft and warm, on hers, and drew back. For a second she thought that would be all. He'd come to his senses; she'd come to hers. But she wasn't trying to hide anything now, wasn't consciously repressing her attraction to him, and he seemed to see the hunger in her expression...the wanting. He smiled into her eyes, tasted her lips once more.

Pulling back slightly, he rubbed his thumb along the smooth line of her lower jaw, his forefinger along her full lower lip. "Why didn't you come down to me last night?"

"You knew I was up?"

"I've been in this house alone a long time. When someone else is here, I'm intensely aware of them. Yeah, I knew. So why didn't you come down?"

"You didn't look as if you wanted to be disturbed."

"I was thinking about you," he said. "About how much I want to make love to you. Isn't that similar to what you were thinking? I can tell, Holly. You've been entertaining thoughts of us in bed just as I have."

Her mouth was dry, the base of her spine tingling, but she managed to arch a brow at him. "How can you tell?"

"Haven't you?"

There wasn't an ounce of doubt in his tone. Even burning for him as she was, Holly couldn't resist goading him: "Guess."

He laughed, a low, sexy laugh deep in the back of his throat. "I don't have to guess—I can damn well find out for myself."

Before she realized just what she'd done, he caught one arm around her and pulled her on top of him as he fell backward, landing softly on the rug. Holly drew in a breath at the sensual impact of his solid body under hers; she could feel the bulge of his maleness under her hips, right where she wanted it.

"Discover anything?" she teased.

"Not enough," he murmured, "not nearly enough."

He gave her no time to revel in the strength and hardness of him. He rolled over, and this time she was the one on the bottom, with him on top. She felt the weight of him, yearned to move under him, rhythmically, primitively.

The orange light of the fire glowed on his face. "Are you going to admit you've fantasized about sleeping with me?"

Holly grinned at him, feeling slightly breathless, and warm . . . very warm. "Why should I?"

"Because I'll kiss you until you do."

"Ah, sweet torture. Come right ahead."

"Holly—"

"I admit it, I admit it. But kiss me anyway."

"Ever since you crashed through my ceiling," he said, lowering his mouth to hers, "I've imagined you here, right where you are now."

His mouth covered hers in a blast of heat, his tongue tracing her teeth as she opened her lips. She could feel herself melting into the floor, wanting him. Still deepening their kiss, his tongue plunging into her mouth, he raised himself up slightly off her chest and slipped his hands under her sweater. Her turtleneck was tucked in nice and tight. He moved his palms up the smooth cotton fabric, until his thumbs were under her breasts.

"I think my feet are on fire," she said. She threw her hands up around his neck and threaded her fingers into his thick hair.

He laughed softly, nibbling on her chin. "I don't think I've ever heard that line before. How's the rest of you?"

"Burning, but not in the same way. I'm serious, Julian." She raised her head about half a foot, still hanging on to his neck, and nodded in the direction of her feet, just inches from the burning log. "Look—my socks are going to burst into flame any second."

Julian glanced behind him. "They are a bit close to the fire, aren't they? But I thought that's how you liked it, your feet to a hot fire, ready and willing to face whatever challenge lies ahead. You like living on the edge, don't you?"

"I'd hardly call a storyteller's life living 'on the edge,' although I admit I do yearn for the occasional adventure. What about you? Working in a sawmill can provide a certain edge to life—no pun intended—and buying a house in as bad a shape as the Danvers House has its risks. And living out here in the woods like a damned wolf. Does Millbrook give you all the edge you need in your life?"

"Maybe not," he said, returning his gaze to her, his eyes lost in the shadows, "but it's where I belong."

She nodded, suddenly envious. "What a nice feeling that must be, to belong somewhere. Julian, we'd better stop." She dropped her hands back down and tried sitting up, but he didn't budge. "Really. This isn't going to get us anywhere but into trouble."

"We're adults, Holly. Tell me," he said, not teasing now, "do you want us to stop?"

"Do you?"

"I know I don't want you leaving Millbrook without us taking the chance to find out what we could be together. Is that what you want?"

Again he brought his mouth down close to hers, his hard, warm body nestled into hers. He just looked at her, waiting. She could smell the damp fabric of his shirt, and placed her palms on his upper arms, exulting in the knots of muscle there. She knew she'd made her choice when she'd agreed to spend the week at his isolated house in the woods. With her fingers extended, she slowly brought her hands along his shoulders to his nape and she clasped her fingers. She met his gaze without hesitation or self-consciousness.

"No," she whispered, gently pulling his mouth to hers, "I don't want that at all."

THEY COULD HEAR the fire crackle from up in the loft. "The wolf's lair in the deep dark forest," Holly said, smiling.

Julian laughed. "I sharpen my claws every morning before getting out of bed."

"I believe it. And your teeth?"

"They don't need sharpening." His voice was low as he slid his arms around her waist and brought his mouth to hers, teasing her with a feathery kiss. "As you'll discover."

"I can't wait."

"You don't have to."

He brought his mouth to hers once more in a hungry, passionate kiss that sent waves of longing undulating through her. She parted her lips immediately, searching for his tongue with hers, moaning with pleasure when she found it. He untucked her shirt and slipped his warm hands underneath, sliding them up her bare skin. She shuddered with excitement.

"You feel so good," he murmured, inhaling deeply when he found her breasts.

Slowly, indulging himself and her, he circled each nipple with his thumbs, turning them into hard buds under the filmy fabric of her bra.

"I don't think I can stand this," she whispered.

He grinned. "Do you want me to stop?"

"No . . . never . . ."

He pulled her sweater and turtleneck higher, up to her neck, and she groaned with impatience, peeling them off. She flung them onto the floor. Her hair was wild and filled with static, but Julian didn't seem to notice. His gaze was riveted on her near-naked torso. She could feel her excitement building, just having his eyes on her.

She started to unclasp her bra, but he stopped her. "Let me," he suggested hoarsely, finishing the job himself with trembling fingers. He dropped her bra on the floor. His eyes never left her.

She smiled, moving closer to him. "You have the sexiest voice. Even when you were yelling at the Danvers House and trying to scare an innocent trespasser—"

"Innocent and you are two things that just don't go together."

"Is that so?"

"So you thought I had a sexy voice while you were cowering up in the bedroom with your crowbar."

"Mmm. I thought it sounded delicious. I just wanted to gobble it up."

He laughed. "Who's the wolf now . . ."

His voice trailed off, his eyes clouding with bridled longing, and Holly shuddered, tingling all over with desire. The time for chitchat had passed. She opened her palms on his waist, her fingers splayed on the hard flesh of his back, and pressed herself against the soft, worn fabric of his shirt. She could feel the solid muscles of his chest against her breasts, could feel herself responding, aching for more of him.

They kissed again, deeply.

"You're getting goose bumps," he said, sliding his palms up her bare arms.

"I'm not sure they're goose bumps, but—"

"There're flannel sheets on my bed."

"But no electric blanket."

"I don't think we'll need one."

She brushed one finger across his chin. "I can't imagine we would. By the way... are you prepared for this? I've got the proper equipment in my van—"

He arched a brow. "Equipment? Sweetheart, I can't tell you how ominous that sounds to a man about to make love with a woman."

With, she thought, not simply *to*. "Well, you know."

"I guess I do, but we're all set. No need to go out into a blizzard for any 'equipment.'"

Standing back from him even a few inches, she shivered in the cool temperature of the bedroom. He was right. She was getting goose bumps. She quickly pulled back the blankets and scooted between the flannel sheets, then pulled the covers up to her chin. In just seconds she had the rest of her clothes off and pitched them out onto the floor.

Julian had pulled off his shirt and was working on his pants. His arms and shoulders and abdomen were just as lean and muscular as she'd expected. Inhaling, holding back the waves, she imagined running her hands through the dark hairs on his chest.

"The cold doesn't seem to bother you," she pointed out, hearing a husky quality to her own voice.

He grinned at her as he stepped out of his pants; she could see the knots of muscle in his thighs and calves, a jagged scar across the top of one knee. "Maybe I'm just looking forward to the process of warming up."

In one swift movement, he removed his underpants.

"I guess you are," she replied.

He laughed. "Some things tell no lies."

She shoved over, making room, and he eased under the covers beside her. Already she could feel the heat of his body. When he touched her, his hands were only slightly cooler than they had been, and she rolled onto her back as he rubbed her sides from her hips to her breasts, as though just warming up.

"You're making me hot," she said.

He moved on top of her. "Is that good?"

She wriggled under him, feeling his maleness pressing against her, and draped her arms over his shoulders. "It's wonderful."

His skin was sleek and hard as she ran her palms across his shoulder and down his arm. She exulted in the sound of his soft moan of pleasure when she dropped her hands to his hips, cupped the curve of his buttocks.

"You can't begin to know what you're doing to me," he said, his voice raspy, and dropped his mouth to hers.

Their kiss was hot and wet and hungry, and it went on and on, even as he lowered the length of his body onto hers ... even as he slipped his hands under her buttocks and pressed himself erotically against her. She ached for him, knew she'd never have enough of him. He trailed wild kisses down her throat, searing a path to her breasts, where, slowly and exquisitely, he took the tip of one pink nipple into his mouth. He teased it with his teeth and tongue, sending tremors of desire all through her.

The primitive, rhythmic motion of his hips, his maleness, against her never stopped, never abated.

"Julian . . ."

"I know, darling, I know . . ."

In just a few efficient seconds he dealt with the matter of protection. Then he smoothed her hair with one hand and held her eyes with his, until at last he entered her, cautiously at first, slowly. She shut her eyes, could sense the passion, the thrill of her pleasure, on her face. He had to see it as well. She pressed her hips up into his, drawing him deeper into her, and he responded with a deep, hard thrust that made her head spin with ecstasy.

It went on like that for a long time, time without measure, absorbed in each other, giving pleasure, receiving, joining hearts and souls in a union beyond the physical. She remembered that they had to kick off the blankets; they were getting too hot under them. Remembered feeling the cool air on her, refreshing now, almost erotic. Remembered thrust after thrust after thrust as she cried out with the energy and joy and sheer beauty of her release, and again more thrusts, more cries, as he joined her in a place where neither had been before, not like that, not with that sense of completion and perfection.

She remembered everything, afterward in the silence.

Julian drew her close to him, seemed to know words weren't necessary, not now. Downstairs the fire crackled, and she could hear the dogs sigh, as if they approved. And she thought, feeling drowsy and satiated, *I belong here . . . somehow.*

9

Friday evening before Holly Wingate Paynter's scheduled appearance at the Millbrook Historical Society fund-raiser, Julian had dinner alone at his favorite local diner. He ordered the dinner special, homemade chicken potpie. Holly was off with Beth putting the finishing touches on her plans for her performance. They'd become fast friends over the past week, his sister and his lover.

He winced. *My lover...*

They had had an extraordinary five days together. Monday afternoon after the blizzard, she had sat beside him in the truck while he plowed his driveway. He expected she'd eventually recreate the experience in some fanciful way for one of her stories; she'd asked enough questions about what he was doing. Then Abby and David had showed up with their sleds, and Holly had been forced to admit to the two kids that she'd never been sledding. They fixed that in no time. Julian could still see her wide-eyed look of delight and terror as they piled onto the toboggan and went screeching down the snow-covered path to the brook, coming to a crooked stop at the water's edge.

Tuesday he'd headed to the sawmill, and they had met for lunch in town and gone over to the Danvers House together. He showed her where he'd found the goblets in the old dirt cellar. She admitted—reluctantly—that although there *might* have been a couple of stray golden retriever puppies out at the academy, in fact she hadn't seen any. She'd used them to get herself out of a tight spot with him. He had agreed he had been trying to look intimidating, despite her apparent obliviousness to his efforts.

She did not explain why she'd stolen the goblets, but he didn't tell her he continued to doubt her tale about wanting to "borrow" them for props.

He was waiting for her to try to swipe them again, in fact. The woman was relentless about anything and everything, including making love. And that was no complaint. She was a thoughtful, inventive lover, and he wouldn't trade their week together for anything in the world.

He hated to think that would be all they'd have together. A week. A glorious memory. He wanted more—a lifetime.

But he'd begun to sense a certain restlessness in her spirit. After nearly two weeks in Millbrook, she was ready to move on. Stir-crazy. She made phone calls, wrote, snooped around town and mailed piles of stuff virtually every day. She clearly was working. As she explained to him, she had taken a couple of months from her usually busy performance schedule to pull back and relax, dig into long-postponed projects. Aside from the hastily arranged Millbrook fund-raiser, her next appearance wasn't until April, in Atlanta.

Still, she was ready to roll. Julian didn't take it as a personal offense. Her restlessness was simply a part of who she was—and he'd vowed he would never demand she change or curb it. It would be like asking the wind to stop blowing.

While he waited for his chicken potpie, he headed to the pay phone and dialed Felix Reichman's number.

"Felix—I'm not trying to rush you, but I've got some unexpected outside pressures on me about this goblet thing. You wouldn't by any chance have anything new to report?"

"Actually I've been in touch with a friend of mine at Harvard," Felix said in his precise, unhurried manner. "She's given me a rather interesting lead. I haven't followed up on it yet, so it may be nothing. Apparently she knows of a letter Paul Revere wrote that reportedly mentions the goblets. As I said, it may prove unimportant, but I thought I'd travel to Boston and see for myself."

"Sounds good. Anything else?"

"Nothing you don't already know. Oh—have you heard Zachariah Wingate's great-granddaughter is in Millbrook?"

Julian didn't say a word. Great-granddaughter?

"She's a storyteller."

Indeed she was that. He said, noncommittally, "Is that right?"

"She's quite marvelous, I understand."

"You're sure she's Zachariah's great-granddaughter, not just a distant relative?"

"Oh, yes. I thought it might be advisable to try to discover what happened to Zachariah after he left Millbrook. I realize that's not directly related to the question of where the goblets came from and how they ended up buried in the Danvers House, but I thought perhaps I might discover a few pertinent details that could lead me backward in time, to the goblets. As it turns out, Zachariah ended up in Texas quite broke. He married and had one son, also named Zachariah, and settled in the Houston area. The younger Zachariah had a daughter, who died twenty-three years ago, but not before she'd married and had a daughter herself—"

"Holly Wingate Paynter."

"Correct. She's our Zachariah's only living direct descendant."

Hence, her interest in the goblets. Julian felt his jaw clench. So much for honesty and trust.

"Julian? Are you there?"

"Yeah."

"As it happens, she's performing tonight—"

"I know, I'm going."

"Are you?" Felix sounded amazed.

"Yeah, I get out once in a while. I just didn't realize her connection to Zachariah. Look, Felix, go ahead to Boston and find out what you can about this letter. Keep track of your expenses and I'll reimburse you for everything. And thanks."

"My pleasure," Felix said.

After he hung up, Julian stared at the phone, seeing only Holly's milk-white skin and lying, glittering blue eyes as she blithely lied to him and his sister about being a "distant" relative of Zachariah Wingate. The lady never quit! Yet that determination was part of what attracted him to her . . . made him want to keep peeling back the layers of lies, deceptions, half-truths and defenses, until he came to the real Holly Paynter. He'd had a few peeks at her in the past week. But peeks, he was discovering, just weren't enough.

The waitress hollered at him when his dinner came up, and he slid onto a stool at the counter . . . where the food was hot, the coffeepot always full and the talk of ski conditions, town politics and one pretty strawberry-haired, storytelling Texan.

THE FACTS OF that notorious night at the Danvers House in the spring of 1889 were simple enough. In her stories, Holly never contested known facts—only assumptions.

Earlier in the afternoon on that chilly late March day, Zachariah Wingate, a sixteen-year-old scholarship student at the Millbrook Preparatory Academy for Boys in Millbrook, Vermont, was expelled for being a thief, although no legal charges were brought against him. That night he arrived alone at the Danvers House, amid an elegant dinner party, and requested a private audience with Edward Danvers, the headmaster of the school and a descendant of its founders, and Jonathan Stiles, chairman of the school's board of directors and one of its chief benefactors. Unusual for such a prestigious school, both men were from the local community. So, of course, was Zachariah. Hat in hand, young Zachariah withdrew with the two older gentlemen to the front parlor. An hour later, the boy left and Edward and Jonathan rejoined their dinner guests, never mentioning what they'd discussed with the unfortunate young man.

The next morning, the signed sterling-silver Paul Revere goblets Zachariah had tried to present to the

academy in thanks for its support of his education—
and was accused of stealing—were missing from the
safe at the Danvers House. And Zachariah Wingate had
disappeared.

They were the facts of the case, corroborated by wit-
nesses.

Simple enough.

Before her rapt audience of over a hundred Millbrook townspeople, Holly recreated that night at the
Danvers House, never deviating from known—accepted, *proven*—facts. She helped them envision the
elegance of the dining room and the guests gathered
there, in contrast to the rail-thin, hapless boy, cold from
having walked down from his family's struggling sawmill, a sixteen-year-old who, in trying to find a place
among the elite student body of the Millbrook Preparatory Academy, always seemed "damned if he did,
damned if he didn't." He was likable enough. Gener-
ous. Wanted to do the right thing.

He had believed the goblets had come to his family
from Paul Revere. It was what his father had told him,
what his father had said *his* father had told *him*. And
on like that, back more than a hundred years to the
American Revolution. Zachariah had no reason to
doubt his father's story, no reason to suspect he might
be accused of having stolen the goblets himself, out of
a misguided sense of pride.

It could have happened that way. Or maybe he did
steal the goblets in order to give them to the academy.
Who knew?

Holly never mentioned that Zachariah hadn't left
Millbrook that night with the goblets. She didn't have

to. Everyone in the audience realized he couldn't have. Otherwise, how'd they end up buried in the dirt cellar of the Danvers House for Julian Stiles to find a hundred years later? *That* question Holly didn't touch.

Privately she wondered which of the thieving two—Edward or Jonathan?—that night had realized Zachariah indeed was innocent and there'd be no owner clamoring for the return of the goblets. Which one had swiped them from the safe and buried them toward the day when the other—or Zachariah himself—wasn't around to counter his version of that night? Events must have conspired against the guilty party, because the goblets remained buried until just a few weeks ago. But Holly didn't speculate.

What she did was tell a story, a human story of human fears and weakness—and pride and duty. Zachariah's pride in and sense of duty to his family and himself. Edward's and Jonathan's pride in and sense of duty to the academy and their community. She told the story with anger, with humor, with confusion, with warmth. With believability.

And she never once deviated from the cold, hard facts of the case.

Wisely she slipped the Tale of the Silver Goblets between a funny, fantastic story about balloons and a short, spooky ghost story. Neither did anything to remove the skeptical look from the face of Julian Danvers Stiles, standing in the back of the Old Millbrook Town Hall. Afterward she didn't go out into the crowd as was her usual practice, but let people come to her.

"You were wonderful!" said the first, a young woman with a preschooler on each hand. Holly thanked her warmly, and others followed.

"Just a delightful performance, Ms Paynter."

"Holly—that was fabulous!"

"I laughed until my stomach hurt…and now I've got tears in my eyes. You managed to tug all my emotions."

"Oh, Holly, Millbrook will never look on the Scandal of 1889 the same. Whatever really happened that night doesn't even matter."

"Marvelous. I hope you'll come to Millbrook again soon."

What could be more rewarding than the acknowledgement of a job well done? She'd had her storyteller's burn on tonight. She'd had to do some improvising, but all in all, she thought she came up with a fairly nonthreatening story that related to all of Millbrook the Wingate version of what happened the night Zachariah Wingate and the Paul Revere sterling-silver goblets had disappeared. It might have happened that way; then again, it might not have. She'd made no apparent judgments. In fact, she'd gone out of her way to make Edward Danvers and Jonathan Stiles look less like the villains they were and more like the upright citizens trying to do the right thing that Millbrook residents, then and now, wanted to believe they'd been. Grandpa Wingate would have scoffed at her generosity. Scoundrels, he'd have called them.

"It's good to know," said one elderly gentleman, taking Holly's hand, "the Wingates made out all right and haven't held a grudge all these years."

There was soft, sarcastic laughter behind her, and she didn't need to turn around to know it was Julian.

"Thank you," she said to the older man, "but my interest in Zachariah Wingate is purely professional. My middle name's just a coincidence."

Satisfied, the elderly gentleman made his way back through the crowd.

"You're quite a storyteller," Julian said, his eyes on hers, "but I knew that already."

She decided to take his compliment seriously. "Thank you. Julian—is something wrong?"

"You've been lying to me all along, Holly."

"What?"

"You lied to that old man. You've lied to all of us."

"Julian . . ."

"I'd almost come to believe you and Zachariah were just distant relations."

She licked her lips and found that they were parched; her throat was tight. She couldn't have said a word if she'd wanted to.

"You're Zachariah Wingate's great-granddaughter."

Her natural bent toward self-preservation and her postperformance storyteller's "high" spurred her to action. "Oh, so *that's* what's wrong. I was worried there for a minute. Julian, I was going to tell you tonight. I just wanted to wait until after my story. If I told you beforehand, I was afraid I'd lose some of the spark and energy that I need for a performance. It's difficult to explain."

He didn't look impressed. "You're a pro, Holly."

She wasn't entirely sure what he meant. A pro at lying? A pro at storytelling? A pro who should have been able to tell a lover the truth and still be able to do her work? She bit one corner of her mouth. "It wasn't exactly a lie, Julian. I was . . . saving the truth."

"You're going to start tripping," he said, "over all those truths you've saved."

The arrival of his niece and nephew, boasting to a tagalong friend that *they* knew Holly, spared her from having to come up with a retort. She gave the kids her full attention, feeling Julian's eyes boring into her back. One of the perks of being a storyteller was she could dress to her own satisfaction, which usually translated into comfortable, easy clothes that didn't draw attention to her appearance, and away from her stories. To-night, because after all, she was the first Wingate in Millbrook, Vermont, in a hundred years, she'd opted for a slightly dressier outfit of flowing black skirt, emerald-green charmeuse blouse and great big fake gold earrings. It was too late to change by the time she realized the green of her blouse matched exactly the green of Julian Stiles's eyes. But she felt sure she'd be the only one who'd notice.

Abby and David told her they'd loved her balloon story, and the third kid said he didn't get that stuff about the silver goblets—what were goblets, anyway? Holly laughed, and she encouraged them to think about their own stories, of growing up in southern Vermont, of ice skating in the sawmill parking lot and throwing stones in the mill pond.

Dorothy Windham—Aunt Doe or just plain Doe to most of the town—extricated herself from a group of well-wishers. "Julian, take these children over to the house, will you? And Holly, you can ride with them.

Beth's already there. Tell her I'll be along in a minute. I forgot to invite Dr. Ben, and he can be such a stinker—"

"Invite him to what?" Holly asked.

"The party!" David shrieked. Then he winced, looking mortified. "Oops—sorry."

Aunt Doe laughed. "No matter. Holly, we're just so excited to have you. We planned a small reception for after your performance back at the house."

Holly laughed, truly surprised and more pleased than she wanted to admit. "How lovely."

Julian leaned close and said quietly, "Just consider it a truth we were saving."

HOLLY TOOK THE S-CURVE on Julian's narrow, impossible and totally *outrageous* driveway very slowly. It was darker than the pits of hell out there and as cold as she wanted January in Vermont to get. She didn't relish the prospect of going out of control and pulling a one-eighty. After the reception at the Windham House, she was tired and nervous enough without any extra stimulation.

Push had come to shove with her and one Julian Danvers Stiles.

He had been very decent at his aunt's house. Amusing. Kind. Easygoing with his friends and relatives. Complimentary to her. The picture of the well-bred Yankee gentleman. Handsome and courteous. But restrained. Remote. Distant. It wasn't anything overt, just the cumulation of an evening of small signs. Not once did he goad or tease her, or even doubt anything she said. He had been unfailingly polite.

She could tell he was upset about her being Zachariah Wingate's great-granddaughter and not having told him.

Only once, in a conversation with the executive director of the regional public radio station, had she caught Julian without that tight rein he had on his real emotions. The director was tempting her with notions of putting together her own thirty-minute program, which they could air locally and then syndicate to other public radio stations nationally, when she'd spotted Julian watching her. There was heat in his gaze, and unexpected tenderness. Catching his eyes, she'd smiled; he'd smiled back. But the heat and the tenderness had vanished, and she'd turned away in confusion. She didn't even know how she felt anymore. How could she expect to know how he felt?

Adam Stiles had arrived late, apologized to Holly for having missed her performance, but listened indulgently as Abby and David gave him an elaborate rendition of all the highlights. Then he whisked them off to make their good-nights, and while their great-aunt Doe loaded up goody bags for them, Adam had a few words with his younger brother. Holly wished she'd been in a position to listen in. She was a remorseless eavesdropper—a snatch of conversation here, a tidbit there and she could come away with fresh insights into people and even the launch of a story idea. But Adam and Julian spoke very briefly, and at a guess, sharply, after which they both left. It was Julian's first rude move of the evening: he said only a curt goodbye to his aunt.

"Those two," their sister muttered when they'd gone.

Holly feigned passing curiosity; it bothered her how deep and tenacious her interest in the Stiles family was. "I've never really seen them fight—they get along, don't they?"

"Yeah, they get along great. I think maybe they understand each other too well—or think they do. Each thinks he knows what's best for the other, and neither minds saying what that might be at any given moment. Sometimes," Beth went on, popping a spinach-cheese triangle into her mouth, "They ought to learn when just to butt out."

"Well, it's none of my business . . ."

"Are you kidding? It's every bit your business." She grinned, playing the role of the big-mouthed, unrepentant little sister. "They'd both dump me in the river if they thought I told you. Adam thinks you're under Julian's skin, but Julian's too damned stubborn, or maybe too afraid, to make any kind of real commitment to you because you're a nomad and he's practically a hermit—and Melissa, Adam's wife, hated Millbrook but tried to stick it out and was miserable, which is why, both my idiotic brothers believe, she got killed. Not true. The reason she got killed is that she was going too fast on an icy road and hit a tree. But try and tell them that. Adam's avoiding all women and Julian's avoiding any woman that might want to step foot outside Millbrook once in a while, not that he doesn't. He's just being weird. Anyway, far be it from me to breathe a word of any of this."

"I wouldn't want you to," Holly said.

"Brothers, you know?"

"Not from experience, no, but I've got a good imagination."

"You sure do. I wish I was as quick with a lie as you are—"

"Beth!"

She laughed. "Holly, Holly. Julian told me you're Zachariah's great-granddaughter. I *know* you're after those goblets, and frankly, I hope you get them. Whether Zachariah swiped them in the first place or not, seems to me he got the short end of the stick that night. I think Julian just ought to give them to you."

"He won't—"

"Not a chance, no."

"You didn't happen...um...to see what he did with them?"

"He put them back in that iron box, tucked them under his arm and took them with him."

"Home, you think?"

"Yes, I most definitely do think. I also think he's just daring you to go after them and—"

Holly shook her head, adamantly. "No, your aunt had a cancellation for tonight, and I packed up my van and plan to head out tomorrow."

"Because of Julian?"

"Let's just say it's time to be shed of Millbrook, Vermont."

But it was because of Julian. If he'd reacted differently to her being Zachariah Wingate's great-granddaughter, if he'd given any sign to the rest of Millbrook that he'd become more than a conscientious host to Holly during her stay up at his place—if he'd shown he *cared* about her. No, it was time to move on.

"Does he know you're leaving?" Beth asked.

"I've never made any secret that tonight would be my last night in town."

"If you really want to know how he feels about you," Julian's only sister went on, "just steal the goblets."

Holly had managed a laugh. "You'll testify on my behalf in court if he has me arrested?"

She'd grinned. "Sure."

"I don't know . . . Driving down that driveway of his in daylight's been enough to take ten years off my life. At night—"

Beth interrupted, "Just remember what he tells me: There's nothing out there at night that isn't there during the day."

It was the kind of advice that sounded okay until you were stuck in the middle of the wilderness at midnight, Holly decided an hour later. She pulled over into a small clearing and idled a moment, wondering if the mountain air had made her bonkers. She'd come maybe two-thirds of the way up the interminable driveway. That made about three-quarters of a mile of trees and bleak road up ahead and about a mile and a half of trees and bleak road behind. She refused to contemplate what kind of night creatures might be out and about. *Best just to stick to the plan.* Such as it was. It was more an act of desperation.

If she left Millbrook with nothing else, she had to leave with the goblets. And if Julian decided to come after them . . . and her . . . then so be it. If not— It was a prospect she simply couldn't imagine.

JULIAN COULD FEEL the cold on his cheeks, but the rest of his body was warm enough as he walked through the snow on a path that cut into the woods parallel to his driveway. His eyes and ears were attuned to the night. As his vision adjusted to the darkness of the woods, he could make out broad shapes and silhouettes. He considered using a flashlight counterproductive, an intrusion. His hearing was keener, more careful and deliberate than in daylight. He could hear the sounds of breezes in the leafless trees, the occasional scamper of a night creature.

And the putter of Holly Paynter's van on his road.

He had been out with the dogs for almost an hour, thinking about her. Wishing he'd pressed her to turn down his aunt and stay with him again tonight. He hadn't wanted to be selfish. Staying with him would only make her departure more difficult. And she needed to leave. She was a wanderer . . . and a tale-teller of the first order.

Was she going to leave without the goblets?

He wouldn't bet on it.

"You're playing games with her because of me," Adam had said. "You're making assumptions about her and about yourself based on what happened between me and Melissa. That's stupid and self-destructive."

Adam had never had a problem with being ambiguous. But, Julian wondered, was what he said true?

He heard Holly switch off the van's engine, and the night once more was still. Had she gone off the road? Gotten stuck? Not Holly. She'd just talk her van into getting back onto the road.

She was up to something.

The goblets...

Softly calling the dogs, Julian left the path and felt his boots sink into the deep, virgin snow, up to his knees. It wouldn't be easy going, but it'd be quiet and fast.

He'd catch up with her in no time.

10

TELLING HERSELF it wasn't *that* cold out, Holly flipped on the flashlight she'd bought to replace the one she'd lost during her foray into the Danvers House. The thin beam of light illuminated only a limited path, but she pointed the flashlight down and focused its beam on the packed snow, ice and dirt that was Julian Stiles's driveway. Whatever might be lurking in the darkness around her, she told herself, wasn't her problem. Her world was reduced to the two or three yards in front of her. She moved quickly, the light wind numbing her cheeks, and she was glad she'd had the wherewithal to change into corduroys, turtleneck, sweater and heavy socks and her gum shoes. The Vermont woods at midnight were no place for silk charmeuse.

Or you, she added silently. *If anyone'd told you two months ago you'd be out here tramping around in the wilderness you'd have laughed yourself silly.*

And yet, here she was. Not laughing, for certain. Some kind of inexplicable feeling, some weirdness, even desperation, had gripped her since she'd first spotted that piece on the rediscovery of the goblets. It was as if her life would never be the same until she came to Millbrook . . . and even then. A part of her seemed to be in this town. She'd sensed that much, if vaguely, since childhood and Grandpa Wingate's earliest tales of the evil doings of Edward Danvers and, to a slightly lesser extent—in that he didn't actually do the expelling—Jonathan Stiles.

She scoffed, muttering aloud, "That's the kind of thinking you do when your brain's operating in below-freezing temperatures."

She walked faster, hoping her footsteps would drown out any spooky noises coming from the darkness. Any creatures lurking beyond the range of her flashlight doubtlessly were more frightened of her than she should reasonably be of them. Bears would be hibernating. What else could there be? Birds, maybe a few raccoons...bobcats. She'd hate to meet up with a bobcat. And fox. They didn't hibernate. Deer—bucks could be fierce.

"Lions and tigers and bears—oh my!"

But she was no Dorothy and this no Land of Oz. Holly could hear her words and her laugh echo hollowly in the night. The house couldn't be too much farther. She hoped Julian would be asleep, and she could sneak in and out without his noticing and— *No, you don't.* She shuddered at her own confusion. Her plan was a sound one—it'd work. She could swipe the goblets and slip out of Millbrook for good.

The question was, did she want her plan to work?

Her toes were getting cold. She picked up her pace...and slowed down all at once, sure she'd heard something. Her heart pounded, and she stumbled, her knees wobbling, her imagination running wild.

Then a creature shot out across the road, and then another, and she jumped, so startled she couldn't make a sound, expecting she was going to be attacked and ripped to shreds at any moment.

"Pen— *Ink!* Over here."

Julian's voice, low and commanding, came from the darkness off to Holly's left, but the two dogs had already vanished into the woods on the opposite side of the road. Holly scanned the woods with her flashlight until its beam fell upon Julian's dark figure climbing over a snow-covered stone wall. He jumped down, landing softly beside her.

"Whoa—turn that thing off. You're wrecking my night vision."

Holly kept her flashlight on. "Hello."

"I guess that's a fairly neutral way to open up a conversation in the woods in the middle of the night. Sorry about the dogs. They must have smelled a rabbit or something—maybe a rat. Anyway, I wasn't trying to scare you to death."

"You didn't," she said, her heart still pounding from the adrenaline rush. "You only scared me half to death. I didn't know what in blazes was coming at me."

He put one gloved finger on the end of her flashlight and pushed it aside, so it wasn't shining in his face. "A guilty conscience at work. What're you doing out here?"

"Walking to your house. My van . . ."

"Your van's fine. Don't try to tell me it broke down because you obviously keep that thing in perfect running condition. And I heard you, Holly. You came to a nice, neat, *intentional* stop."

She sighed, feeling less cold. "So?"

"So you came back for the goblets, didn't you?"

"Why are you always so suspicious?"

"Because I still can't figure you out."

"You think this week's been nothing but a ploy for me to get my hands on the Wingate goblets, don't you?"

"No, I don't," he said. "I do think, though, that you've a deep, personal commitment to the *Revere* goblets that might cloud your judgment."

Holly sighed. Why did she feel exhilarated instead of trapped? *Madness.* She went on, "Okay, maybe I haven't been altogether straightforward with you—"

"That's an understatement, sweetheart."

"Well, I never expected to go to bed with a man who has Danvers and Stiles blood running through his veins. It's making me crazy, okay? I—Lordy, I don't know *what* I'm doing." She broke off, pointing her flashlight straight down at the ground, so that only a small circle beside her feet was illuminated. "I don't think you do, either."

"You and my brother agree on that," Julian said, his voice low and warm as she shivered. "I haven't had a minute's peace since you almost fell on my head."

"I haven't had one since I spotted that article on the goblets."

"You're cold. Let's go inside and get warm by the fire and talk. Come on, we can take your van the rest of the way."

She touched his arm. "Maybe I should just go on back to town."

Although the light wasn't on his face, she could feel his eyes on her, and he covered her hand with his. "Is that what you want?"

"No, I guess it isn't. But you drive, okay? You know the road better than I do."

"Whatever you want."

His voice matched the quiet and the depth of the woods, soothing Holly's taut nerves. She turned back toward the van and raised her flashlight, but Julian urged her to switch it off. She complied.

"Just stand here a minute," he said. "Let your eyes adjust."

"I don't know if I want them to. It's pretty creepy out here."

"Nothing out here that's not there in daylight."

"So your sister tried to tell me." She frowned. "That's not all that comforting a thought, you know. I still think you must be part wolf."

His laughter licked her spine, down low. "Hold that thought."

Her eyes adjusted gradually to the lack of light, and she began to see silhouettes of trees against the starlit sky and the dark path of the narrow road slicing through the woods. Beside her, Julian neither moved nor spoke. They stood together, listening to the wind in the leafless branches of the trees.

Finally Julian whispered, "Not a bad place to be, is it?"

She shook her head. "No, it isn't—it's quite a wonderful place to be." She could hear the emotion in her voice, knew the night was working its magic on her. "I'm ready. We can go."

His well-developed night vision and familiarity with the road to his advantage, Julian guided her with a hand lightly pressed to her shoulder. She didn't mind. Independent though she was, slipping on the ice and falling on her behind and having to be carried out of there would have been a far greater indignity. She preferred to think she had the strength of character to accept another's greater experience at such moments.

Also, she liked the feel of his hand on her. His closeness. She wasn't thinking ahead, plotting and scheming, just enjoying the moment.

By the time they reached the van, its toasty warm inside had cooled to nearly match the outside temperature. Holly rubbed her gloved hands together, shivering now that she wasn't moving. Julian started the engine, but the heat was still on high and gusts of cold air blew in their faces. She reached over and cut off the fans until the engine warmed up.

"We can warm up back at the house," Julian said.

"The sooner the better."

He laughed softly. "Darling, as tempting as you are and as much as I plan to make love to you in this van one of these days, the thought of jumping bareassed into that cot of yours—"

"Why, Julian Stiles, I was just thinking about my frozen fingers."

"Good point. We'll have to warm up your hands before we work on warming up the rest of you—or especially me. Cold hands could cause some real problems."

She laughed. "The mind you have, mister."

As it turned out, her hands warmed up quite fast and proved no problem whatever. They made love in front of the fire, slowly, silently, not wanting to destroy the passion and tenderness of the moment with talk of sterling-silver goblets and a hundred-year-old scandal and a wanderer and recluse who wanted to be together, had to be together, yet didn't know how, except this way, just for the moment.

Curling up under the afghan with him, Holly felt the heat of the fire on her toes and knew the snatched moments would never be enough—not for him, not for her. But could she ask herself to give up who she was for him? Could he ask the same of himself? No, she thought, I don't want him to change . . .

She drifted off to sleep, hoping her dreams would provide an answer.

THE COALS IN THE FIREPLACE were still warm when Julian came downstairs just before six. He restarted the fire, let out the dogs and put on a pot of coffee. There wasn't a sound from the loft; they'd made their way up there sometime before dawn. He'd awakened to find Holly's long, bare leg thrown over his and the scent of her strawberry-red hair in his nostrils. He could still taste her. It had been all he could do not to make love to her again.

But in the cold before sunrise, common sense had prevailed.

He wasn't going to destroy Holly Paynter. She was leaving Millbrook today, and he wasn't going to stop her.

When the coffee was ready, he poured himself a mug and sat by the fire, on the floor. He could see her smile and her so-blue eyes and feel her smooth skin under his hands. He would never forget their nights together. Never.

He could hear her stirring upstairs, wondered if she was having the same attack of clear-headed thinking he'd had. It was one thing in the heat of passion to decide to go for the moment. Quite another to wake up and consider the future. He had no regrets about their week together. The thought of Holly's departure filled him with sadness and anxiety, but he was coming to look upon it as another step in their developing relationship. An uncertain step, to be sure. He didn't know whether they could survive it. But there was no avoiding it. He knew that now.

She leaned over the loft railing, her tangles of strawberry hair flopping into her face, her eyes shining. "Morning—do I smell coffee?"

"You do. Come on down."

"Mountain man hours," she grumbled good-naturedly, and he could hear her skipping down the stairs.

There was no indication in her gait, her voice or her face that she'd had a similar attack of coldhearted rationality.

"Don't get up—I'll fetch my own coffee."

She padded across his living-room floor to the kitchen wearing only knee socks and his navy chamois shirt, not very well buttoned up. *You're doomed, my man.* Julian thought, steeling himself against his all-encompassing attraction to her.

"I've noticed this place stays pretty warm," she said, emerging from the kitchen sipping from his biggest mug. "Is that because of its design or because it's so small?"

"Both. Holly—"

"I haven't been so warm this time of day since I left Florida." She settled down beside him, straightening her legs so that her toes were close to the fire. "'Course maybe the temperature in the house has nothing to do with it. You're looking awfully stern this morning, Julian. What's up?"

"Maybe I'm a bear when I get up."

"A wolf at night, a bear in the morning—interesting metamorphosis."

"If you say so." Then her eyes narrowed, and she peered at him closely, suddenly realizing they weren't having an idle, bantering conversation. "Julian, what's on your mind?"

He forced himself not to look away, to meet her gaze dead-on. "I think you should stick to your original plan and leave Millbrook this morning."

"Yes. But for whose sake, Julian—yours or mine?"

"Yours—and mine. Holly, your life's on the road, not here in Millbrook. You said yourself you're a wanderer. Don't change because of me. And don't ask me to change, because I know I can't. My life's here." He was hurting inside, more than he'd have ever thought possible. "We could go on like this for another week, maybe two, maybe even a month, but you've got your life to live and I've got mine."

"No trying to build a life together?"

"I'm not saying that won't happen in the future, just not right now. Yeah, I'd like to think what we've started here is the beginning of a process, but who knows? I can't predict how you're going to feel when you go back to your world, and God only knows how I'm going to feel when you leave here. I do know, though, that what we've created is artificial—we've both put our lives on hold this past week. I need to know what happens when you go back to your life as a storyteller and I go back to being the Millbrook recluse."

"I understand," she said quietly... but there was something about her tone that made Julian eye her more closely. And he saw not confusion or hurt, but determination. The kind of grit that had brought her to Millbrook after the "Wingate" goblets to begin with.

He was hard-pressed to keep his relief to himself. Holly Paynter was no more finished with him than he was with her. But he said levelly, "I'm not going to beat a dead horse with this. All the discussion in the world can't change what both you and I know has to happen: you've got to leave Millbrook and go on about your business."

"That's what you want, is it?"

"Yes."

"Bull," she said, rising smoothly with her coffee.

"Holly—"

"I'm going to get dressed and get out of here, just like you say. What you're doing, Julian Stiles, is throwing me out."

"That's not true. We're discussing—"

"We're discussing you throwing me out is what we're discussing. What all this talk boils down to is you want me out of here. And I'll go—I might even agree with you, you know, but I *hate* being told what to do. Why do you think I'm my own boss?"

"I'm not trying to tell you what to do . . ."

"And if I say I want to stay?"

"That's not a good idea and you know it."

"There, you see? I'm outta here. And I'll tell you one other thing, buster." Her quiet determination had vanished, and she marched across the rug, glancing over her shoulder as she came to the stairs. "Next time, *you* can come after *me*."

Julian almost smiled. *That's the whole idea.* "Admit you're stir-crazy, Holly."

"Okay. I'm stir-crazy. So what? I'm a big girl. Yeah, I'm a wanderer, but I'll tell you what I'm not, and that's your dead sister-in-law Melissa Stiles. I'm not the tortured city girl who married your brother and tried to live a life she hated just to please him. I'm not going to run off a road in an ice storm and get myself killed. When I get frustrated or angry at somebody, I don't take it out on myself. You or Adam or anybody else bugs me, I'll let you know. Now," she said, catching her breath, "when you realize that I'm Holly Wingate Paynter and nobody else and I'm *not* going to turn into a stick-in-the-mud to please you, you can come after me."

Julian twisted his mouth from one side to the other, taking in her outburst with equanimity. Obviously his sister had been doing some talking—dear Beth was anything but a close-mouthed Yankee. And obviously Holly Paynter had been doing some sorting out overnight as well. He gave her a steady look. "Sympathetic, aren't you?"

"Wingates are used to hard knocks. We know how to cope."

With that, she stomped upstairs. He could hear clothes flying and curses and grunts and didn't know what the hell to do. He'd prepared himself for tears and wails. Holly Paynter wasn't an easy woman to figure.

She hadn't finished. "You know," she yelled downstairs, "there isn't a man alive I'm going to turn into jelly over." She leaned over the rail and shook her finger at him. "And that includes you."

"No regrets about this week?"

"Not one. I even learned something."

He couldn't resist. "What's that?"

Back over the rail she came. "A wolf can turn into a jackass in just a few short hours."

He had to bite back a smile. The woman could give as good as she got; she was tough and yet resilient—and damned if he knew anymore if he was doing the right thing. *You are, you are.* But hell. She *wasn't* a Melissa. Was he afraid of destroying her only because of the tragedy that had been Adam and Melissa's marriage?

Holly thumped back downstairs looking a little frayed at the edges, but she raked her fingers through her hair and grabbed her mug of coffee from where she'd left it on the floor by the fire. "I'll send you your mug," she told him.

"Keep it."

"Wingates learned a hundred years ago not to take charity from a Danvers or a Stiles—and you're both."

"I can't deny that, but a mug isn't charity."

"Yeah, well, maybe I'll smash it to smithereens before I get it in the mail."

"I wouldn't blame you if you did."

"I'm a fighter, Julian Stiles," she said, "in case you haven't noticed. As far as I'm concerned, we've only just begun. I guess I'll see you when I see you."

His heart was pounding, every fiber of his body and soul urging him to grab the wild-haired woman and carry her back up to bed. But he'd made up his mind. "I guess you will," he said. "Goodbye, Holly. I won't forget this week."

"Neither will I," she said, but there was nothing wistful in her tone . . . nothing the least bit final.

He heard the kitchen door slam and lay down on his back on the floor, the heat of the fire licking at his feet. Outside, her van roared to a start. He shut his eyes, feeling the hot tears trickle down his temples into the rug. *God, how can I let her go?*

After a while, he made himself get up and head into the kitchen for another cup of coffee. He called the dogs inside. They seemed to give him accusing looks, blaming him for the loss of potential company. He told them to go lie down.

Then he looked around the kitchen, sensing something was wrong. Just guilt over what he'd done to Holly? He leaned back against the counter, sipping his hot coffee. No, something— "My goblets."

They'd been sitting inside the iron case on his kitchen counter when he'd gotten up. Now they weren't.

Holly Paynter was gone, and so were his matching pair of sterling-silver goblets crafted and signed by Paul Revere himself.

"The lying little thief," he muttered, already feeling better.

She had given him his excuse to go after her.

HOLLY GRIPPED the steering wheel and chewed on her lower lip as she headed out of Millbrook, Vermont, and wondered if she'd handled her confrontation with Julian well at all.

Admitting that she had fallen in love with him.

She, Holly Wingate Paynter, in love with a descendant of both Edward Danvers and Jonathan Stiles!

He was hardheaded and compelling and intensely aggravating. He was also exciting in ways she'd never known. A life with Julian would never be dull—but was it possible?

She glanced at the iron case on the passenger seat beside her. Would the goblets be enough to get him to come after her? She wanted him to see what her life was like, to peel back another layer. She wouldn't be easy to find, but she'd leave a trail—just not an obvious one.

If he refused to rise to the bait of the goblets, she thought, she'd just have to devise another plan.

Because the prospect of not seeing Julian Stiles again was untenable. Although she had the feeling he felt the same way about her, she wasn't taking any chances.

ADAM STILES stood back from the huge up-and-down saw on the lower floor of the original nineteenth-century Wingate mill and glared at his younger brother. "You're the biggest damned jackass I know."

"That's twice in one day," Julian remarked dryly, more to himself than his older brother. He hadn't been able to get Holly off his mind, had hardly even tried.

"You ran Holly out of town, didn't you?"

"She left."

"Because you made her."

"Look, Adam—"

He shook his head, cutting Julian off. "You can rationalize all you want, brother. I know what you're doing—what you think you're doing. You figure Holly can't make it here, you won't do to her what I did to Melissa."

"Adam, for God's sake. I don't blame you!"

Adam didn't seem to hear him. "Turned out, Mel and I weren't good for each other. We did everything we could to make the other happy, the end result being neither of us was happy. Now she's dead and I'm missing a hand. Hell, Julian—you booted Holly out of town because you think she can't be happy here, right? Don't you think she ought to make that decision herself? Decide for herself what makes her happy and what doesn't?" Adam sighed deeply, wiped sweat and saw-dust from his brow with a folded bandanna. "She doesn't strike me as the type who's going to try to drag you off to a split-level house in the suburbs, Julian. Maybe she won't want to live out in the damned woods like a weasel, but that's more a matter of compromise than caving in."

Julian thought he preferred being compared to a wolf than to a weasel. "What's your point, Adam?"

He laughed bitterly. "Hell if I know. Julian—what do you want?"

"I want Holly to be happy..."

"That's not a good answer. You're not responsible for her happiness. Listen to me. There aren't any guaran-tees—we've both been around too damned long to pre-tend otherwise. But you gotta take risks. My two kids are worth any sacrifices I had to make, all the pain Mel and I went through. She was fighting more demons than just me and Millbrook. She was a troubled woman, Julian. And her death had nothing to do with me or the kids—or you. It was an accident. It just hap-pened. Yeah, I blamed myself for a long time. I wished we'd had a chance to sort things out before she died, but we didn't. All that's over."

Julian looked at his older brother. "You haven't had anything to do with women since Mel died."

"How the hell do you know? Look, the right woman comes along, I'll know it." He clapped his brother hard on the shoulder. "Go after her, you jackass. Let things work between you if that's what's meant to be. Don't give up on your own happiness just because you don't want to end up being a crotchety old bastard like me."

"Adam, you know that's got nothing to do with it, but I admit I was hoping you'd say something like that. If I'm going to track Holly down, I'm going to need some time off. I wanted to go over the schedule for the next few weeks with you and Beth, figure out when it'll be the least problem for me to be away."

His brother laughed. "Anytime you want to take off, go right ahead. Hell, it's not like you do so much work we're going to miss you around here."

"You are a crotchety bastard," Julian said with good humor. "You know damn well I haven't taken a vacation in two years—"

"People who work need vacations," Adam jibed, but then he looked at his younger brother, his expression suddenly serious. "Listen, Julian, you need me," he said, "I'm there."

"I know that, Adam. Thanks."

11

BEING ON THE ROAD wasn't the same.

Holly sat on the cot in her van with the doors open and the camellia-scented evening breeze floating over her. It was beautiful and balmy in Florida. She'd parked her van in the driveway of the little stucco cottage her friends in Orlando owned. They'd invited her to sleep on the couch, but her van was comfortable enough. And her mood didn't make her the best company. All she could do was think about her trek through the frozen Vermont wilderness two weeks ago.

Two weeks.

It seemed an eternity.

She had resumed the activities she'd planned for her winter break: she was supposed to relax, work up new material, wander around, bask in the warmth of various southern climates. Not until she'd left Millbrook did she begin to ask herself why she'd arranged such a light schedule for herself. Was it fate? Or was she tired of being a gypsy, of zooming from a performance in one city to another performance in another city—of being so tightly scheduled she didn't have time to live? She had reached the point in her career where she could pick and choose. She didn't have to stay on the road constantly. There were alternatives—good alternatives, both for her long-term career and for herself. She could develop new projects...books, cassettes...a radio program for a certain public radio station in southern Vermont.

She had been making a half-hearted job at working up a new idea all evening, but it wasn't going well.

Two weeks and he hadn't found her.

Two weeks and maybe he hadn't even tried to find her.

"Another two weeks," she muttered, "and they'll be hauling you off to the nuthouse."

She hated waiting. Always had. Her natural impatience was what had brought her to Danvers House and the attention of one Julian Stiles in the first place.

What would she do if he didn't come?

How long was she going to wait to find out?

He could find her easily enough, she was convinced, if he tried. All he had to do was call her Houston number; her answering service would tell him where she was staying. She didn't normally give out such detailed information to callers, but she'd had to leave a trail.

She wanted Julian to be able to find her without too much trouble.

With a huff, she gave up on pretending to work and threw down her pen and clipboard.

She thought she heard something outside. A dog, probably. There were enough of them in the neighborhood and they all loved her van. To discourage further effrontery, she pitched a paperback book out the door and yelled, "Go on—shoo! Find a tree."

"What am I now, a gorilla?"

Julian! At the sound of his liquid voice in the darkness, Holly had to restrain herself from leaping up with excitement and glee. Her throat tightening, she said as calmly as she could, "A dog."

"How charming."

He poked his head inside her van, and she inhaled at the sight of his dark hair, his handsome face, his deep emerald eyes, and was pleased that everything about him still fit the image she'd carried around in her mind for two weeks. She hadn't idealized him.

So he's here, at last.

"Did you come for the goblets?" she asked.

"Partly. They are mine, you know."

"Not morally."

"We can argue that point for a long, long time. Don't you want to know what else I came for?"

"Julian . . ."

He climbed into the van, shut the doors, pulled the curtains and came to her on her cot, climbing over her feet. "Take a guess," he said.

She smiled into his eyes. "Why don't you just show me?"

Her voice had cracked, a rarity for her. Julian smiled back as he eased down beside her on the mattress. It was just a hair small for the two of them, which was perfect. He shifted onto his side and stretched out beside her. The evening air was cooling rapidly, but Holly felt warmer than she had all day.

"That confident, are you?" he teased.

She shook her head. "That hopeful."

"I've missed you." His voice was barely a whisper as he lightly skimmed her cheek with one knuckle; his eyes never left hers. "I lie in bed at night, imagining you beside me. In the morning I can hear you laugh and see your strawberry hair in tangles from a night of wild lovemaking. My life's been hell without you, I'll have you know."

"Good," she said.

"Serves me right for telling you to leave Millbrook?"

"Probably, but I was thinking more that my life's been hell, too, without you, and I'm no martyr. I'd hate to think I've been down here pining for you while you were in Vermont having a grand time for yourself. And anyway, we're together now." She grinned, catching his knuckle between her teeth in a quick nibble. "I'm not suffering."

The simmering heat between them bubbled over then, so abruptly, so totally without warning, that Holly gasped at the depth and immediacy of her arousal. She was wearing a rugby-weight sweat suit, but she might have been nude. Wherever Julian's body touched hers—along one leg, her hip, her shoulder— her skin tingled and burned as if he were trailing kisses from her toes to her forehead.

Within minutes, he was.

Words no longer necessary, each sensing the extent of the other's anticipation, they flung off their clothes and started what Holly had dreamed about, ached for, since their first time. She could see Julian was in the same state she was. But he didn't pounce, and she held back, too. Prolonging the sweet torment of their arousal would only increase the potency, the pleasure of their release.

But she couldn't hold back for long.

First his fingers, then his tongue, warm and moist, traced a patch up her calves, along the outside of her knees, then along her inner thighs, until at last he came to the center of her heat. She felt her body convulse with rhythms that were automatic, primal. Then, at the exact moment she could stand it no longer, he moved onto her, coming into her quickly, hard, fully aware that she was at the edge . . . and so was he.

"You feel so good," he said, moaning with pleasure. "I've missed you."

All at once they were falling, together, a wild, slightly dangerous, wonderful free-fall that had her crying out, laughing, holding him until all at once, without warning, they were no longer plummeting, but floating gently back to earth. They landed together, and they might have been in the soft grass of a sweet-smelling field instead of on the narrow cot in her van. Closing her eyes, Holly snuggled up to his warm body.

"There's never been anyone in my life like you," he whispered into her hair. "You're it, darling. You're all I want."

Sometime later, hours or perhaps only minutes, they came together again, more slowly, with beauty and tenderness, whispering love words, showing each other where to touch, to kiss, to press, opening up in ways they hadn't before.

"We'll find a way to be together," Holly whispered. "We have to."

They were her last words before falling asleep to very sweet dreams. . . .

THEY HAD AN ENORMOUS breakfast at a local restaurant crowded with tourists, and they laughed and talked about nothing important, just what people were wearing, the beautiful weather, how great it felt to be together. Afterward, they headed back to her friends' house. The day was clear and warm, a hint of the ocean in the soft breeze. Holly's friends had gone off to work, and she and Julian sat out on their porch, enjoying the sunshine.

Without fanfare, he told her, "I've got a flight back home at noon. I'd better call a cab."

Holly made no comment.

"I'd planned to take off a couple weeks so we could wander around Florida together, but one thing's led to another with this academy property—and we're swinging into full gear on the Danvers House. I tried to drop everything and go, but I have responsibilities to meet."

"Don't feel guilty, Julian. Your sense of responsibility's one of the qualities I most admire in you. You don't have to apologize for not leaving your brother and sister in the lurch."

"It's just that I have to plan time off . . ."

"Right. I understand."

"Do you?"

He looked so hopeful, and she smiled. "Yes."

He sighed. "Adam, Beth and I have an important meeting tomorrow about the academy property. I have to be there."

"You love your life in Millbrook, don't you?"

He didn't even hesitate. "Not more than I love you."

"But Millbrook's something I can't—won't—ask you to give up, not for me. It's a part of you, same as story-telling's a part of me."

"And wandering?"

"Maybe. I don't think I could give up the road altogether, but it's not the same anymore and hasn't been for a while, even before I met you. I'm looking into alternatives, new adventures—"

"Not because of me, I hope."

"Not entirely. I've always wanted some roots, some stability—a sense of place. I've been looking for that since I was a kid, way before I met you. Now you're in the mix, and yeah, you could affect the choices I make. Why shouldn't you?"

"Because they won't last," he said.

"What," she said, "you want me to be totally selfish? A relationship's a balancing act. I'm not going to do *all* the giving, but I'm not going to do all the taking, either. Julian, I admit I'm new at this. A couple a years ago if somebody'd told me I'd be falling in love with a moun-tain man from Vermont—never mind a cursed Dan-vers-Stiles—I'd have laughed myself into a coma. If somebody'd told me I'd ever get sick of the road, I'd have hooted." She gave him a long look, melting with her love for him. "But things change."

They left it like that, unsettled, the commitment to each other apparent but not the means to make it work. There was no doubt in Holly's mind: Julian would leave her no matter how much he loved her before he'd do anything that he felt would make her miserable, or destroy her, in the end.

The question was, would he be willing to let her make any sacrifice at all to work things out between them?

Would she be willing to let him change for the same reason?

Holly refused to let Julian take a cab. She drove him to the airport, kissed him goodbye with promises of seeing him again soon and watched his plane take off before she headed back into town, feeling faintly sad and very, very lonely.

That evening, after a barbecue with her friends, Holly contemplated her alternatives while she watched the sun set. When she went back to her van, she opened up the iron case, just to touch the silver goblets in an attempt to feel closer to Julian.

Only the silver goblets weren't there.

"The bastard stole them!"

She couldn't have been happier. That was his challenge . . . his plea. Come back to Vermont, his thievery was telling her. Come back and let's try. We've got to be together. We've got to find a way.

How could she resist?

FROM THE OUTSIDE, the Danvers House had changed little since Holly had first trekked across the snowy football field. Vermont was between snowstorms; the fields were dotted with patches of bare, flattened, dead grass, a not-entirely picturesque prelude to spring. The day was overcast and drizzly, nothing approaching the sunny Florida Holly had left behind.

She'd made Vermont in three days flat, through rain, sleet, snow, wind and attacks of doubt. What if she'd totally misjudged the situation? What if Julian hadn't issued her a challenge with his theft of the goblets but just wanted the damned things back and an end to their relationship? He wouldn't be the first man to avoid telling a woman straight up she wasn't wanted. Friends she'd visited on the trip north had counseled her to call him up and ask, but she didn't. What fun was there in a telephone call?

And in her heart, she felt she knew one Julian Danvers Stiles. She was just being stupidly paranoid.

Driving past the defunct academy, she had spotted his Land Rover among a quartet of trucks in front of the dilapidated Danvers House. *Nothing* had changed.

Except for one small thing.

He'd added a sign, nothing elaborate, near the front steps that read Soon to be THE SILVER GOBLETS RESTAURANT.

It was as if he was expecting her.

The steps were slick with drizzle and melting ice. Holly had on her trusty gum shoes, but took extra care. She wouldn't appreciate having Julian scrape her off the steps or stone walk. It was going to be difficult enough convincing him that Vermont was where she was meant to be.

The front door was unlocked, and she went right inside. Smells of fresh sawdust, putty and turpentine greeted her. The place was a whirl of sounds and activity, with carpenters at work in virtually every corner. The Danvers House wasn't exactly transformed yet, but it was well on the way. Everywhere were hints of its former splendor.

Holly felt much as her great-grandfather must have felt a hundred years earlier, treading where a Wingate had no business treading.

"Oh, what the hell," she muttered, and proceeded.

She found Julian in the front living room, hunched over a sawhorse table with two other men who looked just as grubby as he did. He had a big hole at the right knee of his jeans and patches on the seat; his chamois shirt was worn through at the elbows. His dark hair was covered with sawdust, and he was using a rolled up bandanna for a sweatband.

Holly thought he looked incredibly sexy.

Turning, he caught sight of her and smiled as if she'd been gone just ten minutes and was expected back any moment. "Hey, there."

"Hi." She felt a little self-conscious, a little school-girlish. "I thought you were going to do the work on this place yourself."

"Changed my mind. I decided it'd take too long—and I had better things to occupy my energies."

"I see." She hoped she did, anyway. "You left Orlando with something I worked very hard to get."

He grinned, playing the game with her; they'd gone way beyond fighting over a couple of sterling-silver goblets. "Love that slippery wording. I notice you didn't say I left with something of *yours*. Like my sign out front?"

"Gutsy."

"My tractor beam," he said without regret. "I knew it'd pull you back up here."

"Where're the goblets?"

"In a safe place."

"Ahh," she said, "you don't trust me."

He laughed. "Damn right. How long are you in town?"

"One month, minimum."

His eyes narrowed and he went very still. "And where are you staying?"

"My van." She felt a little light-headed, remembering her last days in Millbrook and where she'd stayed. "I was going to stay at the Windham House, but it would get too expensive."

"Nights are still cold up here."

"I figure if it gets too cold, I'll manage somehow."

"You don't have to worry," he said in a low, deliberately sexy voice, "I won't let you freeze."

She smiled. "I never thought you would."

"Why a month?"

"It's my test. Look, you're busy. I can explain all this later. Are you—do you have any plans for dinner?"

"I do now."

Then, ignoring the carpenters, he held her by the shoulders and kissed her hard, leaving her breathless and anxious for the evening.

"You going up to the house?" he asked.

"I thought I would."

"Careful of the driveway—it's in bad shape."

She laughed. "What else is new?"

TO WHILE AWAY the time, she decided she'd cook. Nothing fancy. Her life on the road didn't leave her much time to experiment in the kitchen. She stopped at Millbrook's one well-stocked grocery store and loaded her carry cart with fresh gray sole, salad fixings, Vermont-made apple-cider vinegar for use in a homemade dressing, a concoction of wild and brown rice and a bottle of a medium-priced white wine. At the local bakery, she picked up a crusty load of French bread and indulged in two fat eclairs—and, optimist that she was, six cinnamon-covered cider doughnuts for breakfast.

You'd better burn a lot of calories while you're here, she thought, heading past Old Millbrook Common and out toward the sawmill. She'd decided against stopping there, opting to straighten a few things out with Julian before she reestablished contact with his family. Just to be fair.

As promised, his damn driveway proved even more miserable than last time. The drizzle had washed the sand off the icy patches, making them downright treacherous, and in other spots the snow had melted, creating deep ruts. She sat up straight and hung over her steering wheel, highly alert. After a half mile or so, she grew accustomed to the unpredictable rhythms of the road and started enjoying herself. Even if she skidded, she wasn't going fast enough to get hurt. And if she got stuck, she got stuck. She was dressed for the weather, and in any case, it wasn't so cold out that she was worried about walking a mile or two to the house.

The dogs were inside on the rainy day, but they greeted Holly warmly, remembering her. She found some dog biscuits in the cupboard and gave them a couple, glad for their company, their welcome... the sense they gave her that she belonged there. Within minutes she had a fire going in the fireplace, Miles Davis on the stereo and a start on dinner.

By the time Julian rolled in, she was humming to herself and thoroughly indulging her domestic mood. "It must be months," she told him, "since I last set a table. Everything's ready to go, but there's no hurry."

"Good, I'd like to take a shower first."

"By all means."

The bathroom was downstairs, just off the kitchen. He peeled off his chamois shirt, leaving a sweaty T-shirt underneath, and headed down the short hall.

"I searched the place for the goblets, you know," Holly called to him.

His broad back to her, he laughed. "Didn't find them, either, did you?"

"Nope. Got 'em stashed in a bank vault?"

"Better than that. They're with a friend of mine."

"Oh?"

"An expert in New England history named Felix Reichman." Off came the T-shirt. "You'll meet him sometime."

"Is he writing up the blurb for the back of your restaurant menus?"

"He's providing the facts, but he won't do the actual writing—he's not one to limit himself to five hundred words or less."

Holly scoffed. "Facts, huh?"

"That's right: the whole truth and nothing but the truth."

He turned around, facing her, and unable to stop herself, her gaze drifted over his strong shoulders and flat, muscled abdomen. It was enough to make her forget what they were talking about.

"Nothing more complicated than the truth," he said.

"Or more subjective," she added, her mouth gone dry, her skin suddenly highly sensitized. She'd never get enough of this man. Never.

Apparently unaware of the state she was in, he disappeared into the bathroom, shutting the door behind him. Even the short time she'd spent in Vermont had taught her that primary lesson of northern winters: keeping the door shut cuts down on drafts and makes the bathroom warmer upon exiting the shower.

She heard the water come on. Imagined it streaming down his back. Felt her mouth on his, her breasts pressed against the slick wetness of his chest . . . *I can't stand this.* Dinner would keep, she decided, already in the hall and heading for the bathroom.

"I feel a draft," Julian said, teasing, when she opened the bathroom door.

She shut the door quickly and pulled back the shower curtain. "Just me."

Lathering up his hair, he grinned at her. "Better than one of the dogs. You're going to get wet standing there."

He leaned back into the shower to rinse his hair; she watched the suds melt into the water and stream down his back and front, down to his toes. "Unless you want to come in with me."

"That's sort of what I was thinking."

He grinned. "Sort of?"

"Exactly, then," she admitted, grinning back.

Pulling shut the shower curtain, she quickly slipped out of her clothes and left them in a heap alongside his. The bathroom had already steamed up; she could feel the warm moisture on her skin. She stepped into the shower, at the end of the tub, the hot spray catching her on her breasts, further sensitizing them. The smoky look in Julian's eyes told her he'd noticed. He took his natural sponge, held it just under her chin and squeezed, the warm, soapy water trailing down her front. He pulled back and wetted the sponge again, squirted on a dollop of shower gel and worked it in. Then slowly, exquisitely, he massaged her body with the sponge, from her neck to the very tips of her toes.

"I've imagined doing this to you," he said. "It's gotten so I can't take a shower without getting all fired up."

"Fine by me."

"Yeah, I didn't think I heard you protesting."

When he finally finished, she was burning with desire, her skin so sensitized the tiniest drop of water seemed to sizzle when it touched her, like on a hot griddle. And she still had to rinse off.

"Shall I help?" Julian asked.

Switching places with her, he adjusted the shower head so the flow hit her full force. It was all she could do to remain standing. Then, in a further delicious assault on her nerve endings, he used his palms and splayed fingers to smooth away the last of the suds. He began with the flesh just under her ears and worked his way down, over her shoulders and collarbone, lingering on her breasts until she moaned. Then his hands moved over her stomach, her hips and bottom, to the soft flesh between her thighs.

"I can't stand much more," she whispered.

"Neither can I . . ."

But his fingers didn't stop and her moans of pleasure and longing increased, until at last . . . finally . . . she brought herself to switch off the shower. The bathroom was just too small for what they had in mind. They grabbed towels, huge, soft ones, and she shook her head at his offer to dry her off, knowing she was beyond that. Together they ran out into the hall, the cooler air a surprisingly erotic shock.

They got as far as the fireplace. Julian shooed away the dogs and lay back on his towel, bringing her onto him, her knees straddling his hips. His skin was still damp, but he was as ready as she was. They came together quickly, in a single, beautiful movement. Holly shut her eyes, aware of nothing but their lovemaking...the sheer infinity of her love for Julian. They would find a way to be together. They had no other choice.

A long time later, dressed and satiated, they had their dinner and talked about anything that came to mind— the weather, Groundhog Day, renovations on the Danvers House, family, stories, favorite movies.

Finally, over coffee, Julian asked, "What's this about a month in Millbrook?"

"You're convinced I'm an incurable wanderer, correct?"

"You make it sound like a disease. I simply believe you're happiest when you're able to pick up and go as you please."

"And that's something you can't do, given your responsibilities here and your tendency to be a bit of a stick-in-the-mud. You might loosen up a little, but basically, you're not going to change. I'm not saying I can hang out in one place the rest of my life. Travel's a necessary part of my job—of who I am. But I'm looking for someplace I can feel a part of, Julian. Somewhere I belong. I think that's here, with you. And I aim to prove it."

"You don't have to prove anything to me—"

"It's not just you, Julian. It's me as well. You're right. I haven't stayed in one place for more than a few weeks in years. I need to know I can. Wanting to is different than being able to."

He looked at her over the flickering candlelight, his expression a mix of surprise and sympathy. "You're scared, aren't you?"

Her small laugh wasn't very convincing, and she abandoned it. "Yeah, I guess—a little. If I can't do it...if I start getting itchy for the road after just a week or two..." She paused, reining in her thoughts. "I just don't want to lose what we have together. I want to find a way for *us* to work without destroying who we are as individuals."

"We will," he said, leaning toward her, his face lost in the shadows.

"You sound so confident."

"I am. The way I see it, we don't have any other choice."

12

ONE MONTH.

It wasn't going to be nearly enough. Julian wanted Holly Paynter in his life forever. With very little effort on his part, he'd convinced her to abandon her van for his house. Living in her van, after all, was too much like being on the road. She could get confused. If Mill-brook was to be her "test," she should live like a Ver-monter.

He had her out cross-country skiing one weekend, sledding with Abby and David another, wandering around town and out to the restaurant in the con-verted mill another. She would show up at Mill Brook Post and Beam on weekdays and poke around, soak-ing up atmosphere, she'd tell anyone who'd ask, never explaining precisely to what end. Sometimes she'd meet Julian at the Danvers House, and they'd check up on the plumbers, electricians and carpenters together, or do a little work, or argue about the name he and his friends had chosen for the restaurant. When they dis-covered his sign had been spray painted, she denied she was the vandal. He believed her. Her tactics were sel-dom so direct.

She had lunch a couple of times with his sister, Beth, tea with Aunt Doe, and Adam and the kids invited them over for dinner. Julian introduced Holly to his friends, who quickly became her friends as well, and to the neighbors at the end of his driveway, not that far away, he explained, not even two-and-a-half miles.

But even as busy as they were, there were seemingly endless hours when they couldn't be together. Holly would stay up at the house alone or head into Millbrook and do whatever she felt like doing. That was the deal she'd made with herself.

By the end of the month, Julian knew she was climbing the walls.

And up to something.

That was fine with him. So was he.

"How do you like springtime in Vermont?" he asked her, one month to the day she'd returned to Millbrook. It was a Saturday morning late in March; they'd stayed in bed late, making love. Now they were lingering over a pot of coffee.

"Just because the calendar says it's spring doesn't mean it's spring," she countered. "There's still snow on the ground!"

"Corn snow. It's qualitatively different than the snow that's on the ground in the dead of January. And there's not that much of it left. Up here, sure. We're in the woods and fairly high, but in town—hell, daffodils'll be blooming before you know it."

"When they are, I'll call it spring."

"First day I sink up to my shins in mud, I say spring's come."

She laughed. "Then I guess it's spring all right because I swear I'm going to sink up to my *neck* in mud on that blasted driveway."

"Keeps life interesting."

"That it does. Julian . . ."

"Come on, let's go down to the brook. It must be fifty-seven degrees out there already—perfect March weather."

She sighed, not arguing, and they put on their mud boots and jackets and headed outside. Pen and Ink trotted along ahead of them. The path down the hillside was so muddy it was unpassable, so they went through the "corn snow" in the woods. The winter runoff had caused the brook to rise over its banks. The clear, cold water rushed over the rock-studded streambed.

"In summer," Julian said, "the water comes through here at barely a trickle. You can sit out on that rock in the middle and read a book."

"Sounds lovely."

He smiled, believing her. "It is, until the mosquitoes find you."

While she stared out at the brook, he loosened up a stock in the slowly melting snow and pitched it into the water, watching it float downstream, toward the river. One way or another, he thought, everything's connected.

"Getting restless?" he asked.

"No—it's beautiful here."

"That's not what I mean. Your month's up. Holly, I know you're stir-crazy. Hell, *I'm* climbing the walls.

You've been in Millbrook four weeks straight, it's spring, the weather's getting warm—it's okay to feel like breaking loose."

She looked at him, squinting her vivid eyes in the sunlight. "What do you usually do this time of year?"

He lifted his shoulders. "Tap trees for making maple syrup. Adam, Beth and I've been doing that since we were kids, and now Abby and David are into the act. But sap collecting's already begun. I decided to skip it this year."

"Because of me?"

"Because of both of us."

She turned, looking back down at the rushing brook. "I don't want you to change your life because of me."

"Now you sound like me. Fair play's turnabout, Holly. To build a life with someone else—anyone— means the life you had before is going to change. The trick is to be ourselves, to fulfill our own needs, without destroying anyone else, especially the person we love most. We can be strong and independent and still be together."

"That's possible, you think?"

"It has to be possible, is what I think."

She nodded. "I agree, but . . ."

"But you've got itchy feet and a series of storytelling engagements in Atlanta the first week in April."

"I've loved every minute I've been in Millbrook—"

"I know you have. I also know you'll go bananas if you stay here much beyond another minute."

"That's overstating the case."

"Not by much."

She didn't reply, instead bending down and working her own stick out of the snow, pitching it into the water. Hers snagged in a mass of dead leaves caught on a fallen branch, then freed itself and went zipping along downstream. She blew on her hands, cold from the snow.

"Holly," Julian went on, choosing his words carefully, "I have a confession to make."

She gave him a sharp look that softened almost at once. "What is it, Julian?"

"I've had your van worked on."

The softness in her expression changed to amused suspicion; she no longer suspected him of being capable of doing anything truly rotten. "My van? What did you do, disable it so I can't go anywhere?"

"Tempting as that was," he said, "no. I made a necessary adjustment so *I* could go somewhere in it with you."

Then, before she could badger him with questions, he grabbed her hand and they ran up the hill together, slipping and sliding in the melting snow and mud. She called him crazy, a maniac, a sexy mountain man, a damned wolf since he was so good moving through the woods, and would he *please* slow down. He did, reluctantly. His heart was pounding not with exertion, but anticipation. *What if being on the road was just her way of being alone?* He didn't think it was. Nothing in their time together had suggested that was the case. And yet he worried. *Not for long—you're going to find out, the hard way.*

Her van was parked off to one side of his driveway, apparently unmoved since her arrival in Millbrook.

He'd urged her to toddle around town in one of his four-wheel-drive vehicles, and she'd complied.

"Have a look," he said.

The doors were unlocked. Eyeing him suspiciously, she opened up and crawled in back while he waited nervously outside.

In a few seconds he heard a tremendous hoot of pure glee.

"You *scoundrel*!" she yelled, delighted.

He poked his head inside. "I gather you don't object?"

She was stretched out on the new sofa he'd had installed. It opened up into a full-size double bed—a step up from her too-narrow cot. "At least I know what's important to you," she said, grinning.

"You are, love," he said, and he crawled into the van, shut the door and helped her initiate their new bed.

THAT AFTERNOON they hit the road for Atlanta. Before they'd left, Holly had interrogated him about everything. What about the dogs? Beth would take care of them. The driveway, should it snow again? The neighbors. The Danvers House? His friends—now *their* friends—who were starting the restaurant would supervise while he was gone. His work at the sawmill? He was due a vacation, despite Adam's workaholic example. And Adam? Julian was going with his brother's blessing.

"Holly," he'd told her, "I've taken care of everything."

"Quite the plotter you've become."

"I've learned a few tips from the master plotter."

Who, he reminded himself as they headed south on the interstate, hadn't admitted to what *she* was up to. But that was all right. They had all the time in the world; he'd just wait.

THEY WERE BACK in Millbrook by the end of April. The buds were coming out on the trees, spring flowers were blossoming everywhere and Julian's driveway was dry and easily passable. Spring was Holly's favorite season, and she didn't mind experiencing it more than once a year. She breathed in the fresh, warm air as she carried the box of mail the neighbors had collected into the kitchen and set it on the counter. Julian followed with a couple of bags of essential groceries.

Halfway down the box was the large manila envelope she was looking for. She tore it open at once. "Perfect."

"Reading my mail?" Julian asked, unconcerned.

"Uh-uh. Reading mine. It's something I had sent in care of you."

"Anything interesting?"

"A contract for a radio program I proposed—it's something I've wanted to do for a while, but it requires cutting back on my travel and I wasn't quite ready for that."

Julian peered over her shoulder. "That's the logo of the local public radio station."

"Uh-huh."

"Holly—"

"They've agreed to my proposal and arranged funding. We've got a few details to iron out yet, but basically, I'm all set. What do you think?"

"I think," he said in an ominous tone, "you're a big schemer who could've told me about this *weeks* ago—"

"I like surprises," she countered.

He was about to go for her when they heard the telltale sounds of a vehicle bouncing down the driveway. Out that far, the arrival of company was great excitement. The dogs started howling and both Julian and Holly looked out the window.

"Felix," Julian pronounced.

"Your New England historian?"

"I'll bet he's finished his report on the goblets."

Intrigued and somewhat apprehensive at Julian's obvious optimism, Holly greeted Felix Reichman warily, her Wingate paranoia clicking into gear. She wasn't going to let the goblets stand between her and Julian, but still. They *did* belong to the Wingates.

Which Felix verified in his report. Holly didn't even try not to gloat.

"As I told you, Julian, I investigated a very interesting letter written by Paul Revere," the historian explained as they sat at the kitchen table, the silver goblets in a neutral spot in the center. "It clearly states that he had crafted a pair of silver goblets for Zachariah Wingate's great-great-grandfather, in gratitude of services rendered during the War of Independence—the American Revolution. The goblets described match beyond a reasonable doubt the pair in question."

Julian scowled. "You're sure?"

"I have copies of all pertinent materials. You can decide for yourself. Now—as for the night the goblets disappeared." He licked his lips and adjusted his glasses, not even glancing at his notes. "Julian, did you know your Aunt Dorothy had had in her care for *years* an untouched collection of letters and diaries from your great-grandfather, Adam Stiles?"

Clearly Felix didn't approve of such a wealth of information sitting around unexamined, but Julian merely shrugged. "She's mentioned it once or twice. I never thought much about it. I wouldn't call it a collection, just a bunch of old papers."

Felix gave a long-suffering sigh. "That's why you do what you do in life and I do what I do. You see, I've spent the better part of the past month going through the collection, item by item. And I discovered several diary entries I think you'll find most illuminating."

"Apparently Zachariah and your great-grandfather were friends, and Adam didn't appreciate Edward Danvers's harsh punishment for what he, Adam, viewed as an honorable gesture, especially when no proof was forthcoming that the goblets were in fact stolen. Adam was at the Danvers House that evening when Zachariah came to plead his case. He—Adam—had tried to persuade his uncle, Jonathan Stiles, to overrule Edward's expulsion of Zachariah. When Jonathan decided he had to back the headmaster and Zachariah left in despair, Adam stole the goblets and buried them in the cellar, hoping one day to restore them to his friend. But he died before he was able to locate Zachariah, and the goblets remained where they were until you discovered them."

Julian digested Felix's tale in silence, then laughed. "I'll be damned—so Zachariah wasn't a crook."

"I told you he wasn't," Holly said.

"Well, Edward and Jonathan weren't crooks, either, just a little stiff-necked—and my great-grandfather was a *hero.* He believed in Zachariah. Without him, who knows what would have happened to the goblets."

Holly allowed him that point. "Well, I guess we can name our first kid Wingate Danvers Stiles. Imagine what our ancestors would think! Grandpa Wingate will be haunting me yet."

Felix's eyebrows rose. He quickly gathered up his materials, left them for Julian in a neat pile and retreated.

Julian didn't notice. He was busy scowling at Holly next to him at the table. "How can you give a kid three last names? What's wrong with Peter or Jane or something?"

"We could call him or her Win for short."

"Win Stiles? Sounds like a lottery game."

Holly shrugged, undeterred. "We could use my name: Win Paynter. Except we'd have to work in Stiles somehow, wouldn't we? Wingate Danvers Stiles Paynter."

"That's *four* last names."

"But what a monogram. *WDSP.*"

"It's awful. Are you serious?"

She laughed. "No, not about that."

He turned around in his chair and took both her hands into his. "Then about what?"

"Oh . . . you never know."

"That's true, I don't."

"But this time I think you've probably got a fair idea. I mean, why would I be talking about naming babies if I wasn't thinking about *having* babies—about the future." To her surprise, she wasn't nervous at all. She was too much in love, too sure of him and of herself to be nervous. "You know, this is a small town."

He wasn't going to give her an inch. "Seeing how I've lived here most of my life, I guess I know that."

"And at least a third of the town's a Danvers or a Stiles."

"At least."

"People've been talking about us."

"I know. I hear," he went on, "there's a pool down at the diner on our wedding date."

Holly nearly choked. "I hadn't heard that!"

"Adam told me when I called before we left Atlanta. I think he started it, but he'd never admit as much. He says Abby's lobbying to be a junior bridesmaid, David's already figuring out ways he won't have to wear a suit and Beth's drawing up plans to sell us an addition to the house, seeing how I'll be too busy honeymooning to think of such things myself."

"Well," Holly said, "it's even worse than I thought."

He laughed. "Millbrook's been trying to marry me off for years."

"But you've never really been tempted?"

He gave her a long, searching look. "Not until now."

"Julian, are you sure?"

"Marry me, Holly. We'll travel the world together and we'll always have our place here in the woods to come back to. We'll grow together and be together because that's where we belong."

"I'm . . . I'm at a loss for words . . ."

"At first, I'm sure. Just say you love me."

"Oh, I do. I love you."

"And say yes."

She squeezed his hand. "Yes."

And she leaped into his arms, sealing their promise with a kiss while beside them on the table, the silver goblets sparkled in the spring sunshine.

HARLEQUIN Temptation

COMING NEXT MONTH

#277 THE ALL-AMERICAN MALE
Glenda Sanders

Tired of living in a fishbowl, heiress Cassaundra Snow was determined to experience the "real" world. But posing as the all-American working girl led her straight to Chuck Granger, the all-American male—and a *very* real problem. How could she ever explain to her prince that she was actually Cinderella in reverse?

#278 'TIS THE SEASON
Vicki Lewis Thompson

Anna Tilford was longing for one of those storybook Connecticut Christmases . . . ah, the peace. Until she met her neighbor, who was supplying the official White House Christmas tree. Of course, Sam Garrison had more than just a green thumb going for him . . . and those other assets *definitely* disturbed Anna's peace.

#279 LEGENDARY LOVER Renee Roszel

For thirteen years Tessa Jane Mankiller had nursed both a grudge and a grand passion for Cord Redigo. Now that he'd suddenly reappeared, she wasn't sure which response would win out. But either way, Tessa knew she'd never be the same when he left. . . .

#280 MONTANA MAN Barbara Delinsky

Lily had known that starting a new life would be tough. However, being stranded in a blizzard with her month-old baby and a gruff cowboy named Quist was more than she'd bargained for. But just as she was about to succumb to panic, Lily realized that Quist was evoking some completely unexpected and wonderfully distracting emotions. . . .

Especially for you, Christmas from HARLEQUIN HISTORICALS

An enchanting collection of three Christmas stories by some of your favorite authors captures the spirit of the season in the 1800s

TUMBLEWEED CHRISTMAS by Kristin James

A "Bah, humbug" Texas rancher meets his match in his new housekeeper, a woman determined to bring the spirit of a Tumbleweed Christmas into his life—and love into his heart.

A CINDERELLA CHRISTMAS by Lucy Elliot

The perfect granddaughter, sister and aunt, Mary Hillyer seemed destined for spinsterhood until Jack Gates arrived to discover a woman with dreams and passions that were meant to be shared during a Cinderella Christmas.

HOME FOR CHRISTMAS
by Heather Graham Pozzessere

The magic of the season brings peace Home For Christmas when a Yankee captain and a Southern heiress fall in love during the Civil War.

Look for HARLEQUIN HISTORICALS CHRISTMAS STORIES in November wherever Harlequin books are sold.

HIST-XMAS-1

HARLEQUIN'S "BIG WIN"
SWEEPSTAKES RULES & REGULATIONS
NO PURCHASE NECESSARY TO ENTER OR RECEIVE A PRIZE

1. To enter and join the Harlequin Reader Service, scratch off the pink metallic strips on all your BIG WIN tickets #1–#6. This will reveal the values for each sweepstakes entry number, the number of free books you will receive and your free bonus gift as part of our Reader Service. If you do not wish to take advantage of our introduction to the Harlequin Reader Service but wish to enter the Sweepstakes only, scratch off the pink metallic strips on your BIG WIN tickets #1–#4 only. To enter, return your entire sheet of tickets intact. Incomplete and/or inaccurate entries are not eligible for that section or section(s) of prizes. Not responsible for mutilated or unreadable entries or inadvertent printing errors. Mechanically reproduced entries are null and void. Be sure to also qualify for the Bonus Sweepstakes. See Rule #3 on how to enter.

2. Either way your unique Sweepstakes numbers will be compared against the list of winning numbers generated at random by the computer. In the event that all prizes are not claimed, random drawings will be held from all entries received from all presentations to award all unclaimed prizes. All cash prizes are payable in U.S. funds. This is in addition to any free, surprise or mystery gifts that might be offered. The following prizes are awarded in this sweepstakes: *Grand Prize (1) $1,000,000; First Prize (1) $35,000; Second Prize (1) $10,000; Third Prize (3) $5,000; Fourth Prize (10) $1,000; Fifth Prize (25) $500; Sixth Prize (5000)$5.

   *This Sweepstakes contains a Grand Prize offering of a $1,000,000 annuity. Winner may elect to receive $25,000 a year for 40 years without interest totalling $1,000,000 or $350,000 in one cash payment. Entrants may cancel Reader Service at any time without cost or obligation to buy (see details in center insert card).

3. Extra Bonus Prize: This presentation offers two extra bonus prizes valued at $30,000 each to be awarded in a random drawing from all entries received.

4. Versions of this Sweepstakes with different graphics will be offered in other mailings or at retail outlets by Torstar Corp. and its affiliates. This promotion is being conducted under the supervision of Marden-Kane, Inc., an independent judging organization. By entering this Sweepstakes, each entrant accepts and agrees to be bound by these rules and the decisions of the judges, which shall be final and binding. Odds of winning in the random drawing are dependent upon the total number of entries received. Taxes, if any, are the sole responsibility of the winners. Prizes are non-transferable. All entries must be received by March 31, 1990. The drawing will take place on or about April 30, 1990 at the offices of Marden-Kane, Inc., Lake Success, NY.

5. This offer is open to residents of the U.S., the United Kingdom and Canada, 18 years or older except employees of Torstar Corp., its affiliates, subsidiaries, Marden-Kane, Inc. and all other agencies and persons connected with conducting this Sweepstakes. All Federal, State and local laws apply. Void wherever prohibited or restricted by law.

6. Winners will be notified by mail and may be required to execute an affidavit of eligibility and release that must be returned within 14 days after notification. Canadian winners will be required to answer a skill-testing question. Winners consent to the use of their name, photograph and/or likeness for advertising and publicity in conjunction with this and similar promotions without additional compensation.

7 For a list of our most current major prize winners, send a stamped, self-addressed envelope to: WINNERS LIST c/o MARDEN-KANE, INC., P.O. BOX 701, SAYREVILLE, NJ 08871.

If Sweepstakes entry form is missing, please print your name and address on a 3″ × 5″ piece of plain paper and send to:

In the U.S.	In Canada
Harlequin's "BIG WIN" Sweepstakes	Harlequin's "BIG WIN" Sweepstakes
901 Fuhrmann Blvd.	P.O. Box 609
Box 1867	Fort Erie, Ontario
Buffalo, NY 14269-1867	L2A 5X3

LTY-H119

Wonderful, luxurious gifts can be yours with proofs-of-purchase from any specially marked "Indulge A Little" Harlequin or Silhouette book with the Offer Certificate properly completed, plus a check or money order (do not send cash) to cover postage and handling payable to Harlequin/Silhouette "Indulge A Little, Give A Lot" Offer. We will send you the specified gift.

Mail-in-Offer

	OFFER CERTIFICATE			
Item:	A. Collector's Doll	B. Soaps in a Basket	C. Potpourri Sachet	D Scented Hangers
# of Proofs-of -Purchase	18	12	6	4
Postage & Handling	$3.25	$2.75	$2.25	$2.00
Check One				

Name _____

Address _____ Apt. # _____

City _____ State _____ Zip _____

ONE PROOF OF PURCHASE

To collect your free gift by mail you must include the necessary number of proofs-of-purchase plus postage and handling with offer certificate.

HT-2

Harlequin®/Silhouette®

Mail this certificate, designated number of proofs-of-purchase and check or money order for postage and handling to:

INDULGE A LITTLE
P.O. Box 9055
Buffalo, N.Y. 14269-9055